Closer Than Ever

ROBIN JONES GUNN

BETHANY HOUSE PUBLISHERS
MINNEAPOLIS, MINNESOTA 55438

Closer Than Ever
Copyright © 1999
Robin Jones Gunn

Edited by Janet Kobobel Grant
Cover design by Praco, Ltd.
Cover illustration by Angelo Tillery

Focus on the Family books are available at special quantity discounts when purchased in bulk by corporations, organizations, churches, or groups. Special imprints, messages, and excerpts can be produced to meet your needs. For more information, contact: Resource Sales Group, Focus on the Family, 8605 Explorer Drive, Colorado Springs, CO 80920; or phone (800) 932-9123.

A Focus on the Family book published by
Bethany House Publishers
A Ministry of Bethany Fellowship International
11400 Hampshire Avenue South
Bloomington, Minnesota 55438
www.bethanyhouse.com

Printed in the United States of America by
Bethany Press International, Bloomington, Minnesota 55438

Library of Congress Cataloging-in-Publication Data
Gunn, Robin Jones, 1955–
    Closer than ever / Robin Jones Gunn.
        p. cm. — (The Sierra Jensen series; 11)
    Summary: As Sierra and her friends celebrate their graduation from their Christian high school and their acceptance at Rancho Corona University, she worries about the fate of her friend Paul, who may have been lost in a plane crash coming back from Scotland.
    ISBN 1–56179–722–7
    [1. High schools—Fiction. 2. Schools—Fiction. 3. Christian life— Fiction.] I. Title. II. Series: Gunn, Robin Jones, 1955–   Sierra Jensen series; 11
PZ7.G972Cm   1999   98–37607
[Fic]—dc21   CIP
                                                                    AC

02 03 04 05 06 07 08 / 16 15 14 13 12 11 10 9 8 7 6 5 4

To all the Amys I have known.
Please hurry back.

chapter one

*S*IERRA JENSEN DREW IN A DEEP BREATH AND CLOSED
her eyes. The letter she held in her hand brought
news she didn't know if she dared to believe. She
looked again at the thin onionskin paper and the precise,
bold black letters. Yes, it was Paul's handwriting. And the
words were his, too.

> *I've made an adjustment in my plans for the trip
> home from Scotland. I'm flying out of Heathrow on the
> 12th, which will give me a four-day layover in Portland
> before I go to my parents' home in San Diego. So, what
> do you think? Do you have room for one more person
> at your graduation?*
>
> *I'll ring you up—or wait . . . How do you say it in
> the States? Phone you. I'll phone you. No, it's "call,"
> isn't it? Yes, call. (I've been gone too long!) I'll call you
> next week after you receive this, and you can tell me
> what you think. I wanted to see my uncle Mac and find
> out how things were going at the Highland House, so
> I'll be staying the four days with him.*
>
> *Now, Sierra, I want you to be honest with me, as I*

know you always are. (I'm grinning at the thought of your trying to concoct a polite fib. Nearly impossible for you, right?) When I call, I want you to tell me truthfully if you want me at your graduation. I know this is an important time for you and all your friends, and I don't want to interfere with your plans.

"My plans?" Sierra laughed aloud. As she sat curled up on the porch swing on this warm June afternoon, no one was there to hear her. "What plans? A walk down the aisle, a few photos with Mom and Dad. Maybe a dinner with the family. Those are my plans. I have all the time in the world for you, Paul."

She flipped her long, curly, blonde hair off her shoulder and squinted at the sharp reflection of the sun that bounced off the truck pulling up in front of her house. The cab door slammed, and Randy shuffled to the front steps and smiled at Sierra. He held a legal-sized white envelope in his hand.

"Guess what?" he said, adjusting his baseball cap. He grinned his crooked smile and held out the envelope. "It came."

Sierra quickly folded up her letter from Paul. "What?" she asked.

Randy handed her the envelope. Taking it, she noticed that the return address was Rancho Corona University's. Her face turned to Randy, and she expectantly raised her eyebrows. "Well? Were you accepted?"

Randy stood with his arms folded across his chest, waiting for her to read his letter to find out if he had been accepted to the same university she and several of their friends were attending in the fall. Randy had been more excited about the college than almost any of them when they had gone down to Southern California to check it out a few months ago. Sierra had received her acceptance letter a few weeks ago. Vicki hadn't heard yet, and neither had Randy—until now.

Sierra hesitated. He didn't seem too excited. Did that mean he hadn't been accepted? What would she say to him? How could she hide her soaring excitement over Paul's good news if Randy's letter brought bad news? Carefully pulling out the single sheet of university letterhead, she read aloud. " 'Dear Randy: We are pleased to inform you that you have been accepted for enrollment at Rancho Corona.' "

Sierra sprang from the swing. "Yahoo! You did it! This is great, Randy!" She wrapped her arms around him. He stood with his arms still crossed. Sierra pulled back. "What?"

"There's more. Keep reading."

Scanning the letter, Sierra went on to the next paragraph. "Blahda, blahda, blahda . . . 'and we want you to know that your scholarship application for the music department has passed the first round of advisers and now goes into its final evaluation. We should have an answer for you within the next three weeks.' "

Sierra hugged him again, and this time Randy hugged her back.

"This is so perfect! I can't believe it! Aren't you excited?" she asked.

"Of course," Randy said. His expression looked about the same as it always did, and Sierra realized she had never seen Randy particularly emotional about anything—except maybe once when his band had received a good review in a local paper after a performance at The Beet, a teen night-club in downtown Portland.

"We have to tell Vicki," Sierra said, turning around and snatching Paul's letter from the swing. "I'll be right back. I'll tell my mom we're going over to Vicki's."

"I think she's at work," Randy said.

"That's right. It's Tuesday. Then we'll go . . ." Sierra stopped midstep before entering the old Victorian house where her family lived with her Granna Mae. "I know, let's go out to dinner to celebrate! I'll tell my mom we're eating out. Why don't you come in and call some other people to meet us?"

"Where do you want to eat?" Randy asked, following Sierra into the kitchen.

"How about someplace downtown? I don't want to just go for pizza or tacos. This is a big event." Opening the door into the basement, Sierra yelled down the stairs for her mother.

"You think maybe Italian?" Randy asked with the phone in his hand.

"Perfect!" Sierra said, pointing at Randy. "And I think Amy's working tonight, so she'll be there already. Do you think we need reservations? Mom, are you down there?"

"I don't know," Randy said. "What time?"

"Make it right away so we beat the dinner rush. We probably don't need reservations. Just call Amy to tell her we're coming. Maybe her uncle will even treat you to a free dessert when he hears your good news."

Sierra hurried halfway down the stairs and called out again. "Mom?" The light over the washing machine was turned off; the basement was silent. Sierra headed back up and met her mother at the top of the stairs.

Sharon Jensen, a slim woman with an energetic spirit like Sierra's, had raised six children. She should have been used to noise, but she greeted Sierra with a scowl. "What's all the yelling for? I was upstairs with the boys."

"Randy was accepted to Rancho! Isn't that great?"

"Congratulations, Randy!" The scowl disappeared as Mrs. Jensen patted Randy on the back. He was talking to one of their friends on the phone and responded with a smile and a nod.

"And he might receive a scholarship," Sierra said. "The letter said he'll know in three weeks."

"That's great," Mrs. Jensen said. "Good for you, Randy. I imagine your parents must be proud of you."

Randy nodded his head and went back to talking on the phone.

"I received a letter, too," Sierra said, holding up her envelope with stamps from Great Britain. She slid closer to the dining room and motioned for her mom to follow, as if she were about to share a secret. "Guess what? You'll never guess. Paul said he's coming for my graduation." She waved the letter jubilantly. "And he can stay for four days!"

"With us?" Mrs. Jensen immediately asked.

"No, with his uncle Mac. You know, at the Highland House."

"Oh, yes. Of course. Well, that's wonderful news, Sierra."

"I know. Randy and I are going out to dinner to celebrate. He's calling some people, and we're going to Amy's uncle's restaurant. That's okay with you, isn't it?"

"Who's paying?"

"We all pay our own," Sierra said. "We always do." She glanced down at the pair of baggy shorts and T-shirt she had changed into after school. "I wonder if I should change?"

Mrs. Jensen looked at Randy in his jeans, T-shirt, and baseball cap and said, "I think you'll be okay. You could always go someplace a little more casual."

Randy hung up the phone and announced, "Okay. It's all set. Tre is going to finish making the calls so we can pick up Vicki. I think she gets off at 5:00."

"You'd better move," Mrs. Jensen said, glancing at the clock.

"Who's driving?" Sierra asked.

"You are," Randy answered. "I'm almost out of gas, and we might need to give Tre a ride home. My truck doesn't have enough room if I have you and Vicki, too."

"Remember, Sierra," Mrs. Jensen said, "you can take only three other people in your car."

"I know, Mom. Don't worry." Only once had Sierra squeezed five friends into her old, four-passenger Volkswagen Rabbit. Vicki was the one who had ended up sitting in the middle of the backseat without a seat belt. They had gone just seven blocks, but Sierra had felt guilty for days and vowed she would never hedge on her parents' seat-belt rules again.

Sierra led Randy to the coat tree in the front hallway, where she pulled a small canvas bag from the outside pouch of her backpack. It was only big enough to hold her driver's license, some money, and a small container of lip gloss. But that's all she needed, since her key chain latched to the outside zipper. After Sierra tucked Paul's letter into her backpack, she and Randy slipped out the front door.

Brutus, the Jensens's overly friendly, overly slobbery, overly huge dog, watched them with his paws up on the fence that kept him confined to the backyard. He gave a deep "Woof," and Randy went over to scratch his head.

"Come on," Sierra called from the car. She had the keys in the ignition and was ready to go. "Tell the old fur ball your good news, and let's go."

Randy crawled into the car's backseat and closed the door.

"What are you doing?"

He sat in the middle of the seat with his arms spread out, playfully looking down his nose at Sierra. "I feel like being 'Prince for the Day.' Drive me around. I want to see what it feels like. It's not every day a guy gets accepted to college and practically has a music scholarship handed to him."

Sierra laughed and started the car. "As you wish, Your Highness." They both laughed.

"Just make sure you put on a seat belt. You know what my mom said."

Randy scooted to the right side. "Got it on."

"I can't believe I'm acting as your chauffeur." Sierra headed across town to the dealership Vicki's dad owned, where Vicki worked part-time in the office.

They stopped at a notoriously long stoplight, and Sierra spotted a can of soda rolling around on the car's floor. "For your enjoyment, our in-flight beverage service will now begin." She scooped up the can and handed it to Randy.

"What? No ice in a little plastic cup?"

"Sorry, sir. That's what you get for riding economy."

"Aren't you supposed to say, 'As you wish'?" Randy teased.

The light turned green, and Sierra zipped through the intersection. She pulled into a gas station and parked in front of the convenience store. Hurrying inside, she grabbed a cup, filled it with ice, popped a lid on it, and plucked a straw out of a container. She also snatched up a couple of candy bars and paid for everything—all in less than a minute. Stuffing the change into her pocket, Sierra returned to the car, where she found Randy stretched out across the backseat, with his feet propped up and sticking out the opened window.

"As you wished," Sierra said, handing him the cup of ice and the three candy bars. "Enjoy the pampering, Prince for the Day, because this is the last time you'll ever get this kind of attention from me."

Randy gladly accepted the "en route snack service" and offered Sierra first pick of the candy bars. They went on their merry way as Sierra added to her earlier comment. "But you deserve the attention today, so soak it up, buddy."

"I am." For emphasis Randy took a big slurp of his now iced beverage.

When they pulled into the entrance of Navarone's Car Dealership, Randy said, "Isn't that Vicki over there, leaving the showroom?"

Vicki had a distinctive swish to her walk. Today her silky, brown hair was twisted up on the back of her head in a clip, and she carried her dark blue backpack over her shoulder.

"Looks as if we arrived just in time." Sierra honked her car's horn, and it let out a pathetic " 'eep! 'eep!"

Vicki turned around and saw them. She had a concerned look on her face. Sierra pulled up next to her and called out the window, "Hey, Vicki, hop in. We're going to celebrate!"

Vicki leaned into the car and looked at Randy in the backseat. "What are you doing back there?"

"Being Prince for the Day."

"I call him 'Your Highness,' " Sierra added.

"Why?" Vicki still looked concerned.

"Because," Randy said, "I am the proud recipient of an acceptance letter from a certain university and possibly of a scholarship as well. You don't have to bow—at least not this time. You want the other half of this candy bar?"

"Really?" Vicki said, not appearing at all interested in the candy. An even deeper scowl shadowed her delicate features. "You received your letter today, too? And you were accepted for sure?"

"Yep, for sure. It's official."

"Did you get your letter, Vicki?" Sierra asked.

Vicki nodded grimly.

"And?" Sierra prodded.

"My mom called and told me it came, but she wouldn't open it. She said I should be the one to read it. I'm really nervous about this, you guys. If they say no, what am I going to do?"

"They won't say no," Sierra said. "You have to go to Rancho with us. We won't take no for an answer. We'll storm their administration building or something. I'm sure it's an acceptance letter. Let's run by your house, grab the letter, and then all go out to DiGrassi's for dinner. Randy already called some other guys, and they're going to meet us there."

"I don't know. I probably shouldn't go," Vicki said. "I have so much homework."

"Homework?" Sierra said. "Who gave you homework? I don't have any. All we have to do is study for finals next week, and then it's cruise time."

"It's actually some makeup work for Mr. Ellington's class. I'm trying to pull my final grade up, and the paper is due tomorrow."

"It's only 5:00," Randy said. "We won't stay long. You can be home by 7:00. Hop in, and we'll bring you back here afterward."

Vicki hesitated before opening the front passenger door. "As long as I'm home by 7:00. Seven-thirty at the latest."

"Not up there," Randy said. "You have to ride back here with me."

Vicki's worry wrinkles finally gave way to a smile.

"Okay, scoot over, Your Majesty."

"It's 'Highness,' not 'Majesty,' if you don't mind."

"And what exactly would the difference be?" Vicki teased.

Sierra turned her car around and headed for Vicki's house a few miles away. She felt silly being the only one in the front of the car. It was one thing to have Randy goofing off and for her to play along. But now she felt ridiculous driving through town with her two friends laughing it up in the backseat.

In one way, Sierra thought it was great that Randy wanted Vicki to sit by him. Vicki had liked Randy for a long time, but he had always played it cool with her and all the other girls. Randy's treating Vicki a little special in his lighthearted mood was probably a fun encouragement for her.

At the same time, Sierra felt a foreboding sensation. What if Vicki hadn't been accepted to Rancho? Then what? How could they celebrate Randy's good news if Vicki had bad news? A worse thought struck her. How would Sierra be able to make it though her freshman year if Vicki wasn't there? They had talked about being roommates and how they were going to make sure they had several of the same classes so they could help each other with homework. Sierra would feel awful if Vicki weren't accepted. And she knew Vicki would feel even worse.

"You know," Sierra suggested, "we could just go straight to the restaurant, since people are waiting for us. Then you could read your letter when you get home, Vicki." Sierra glanced in the rearview mirror to see if her feeble suggestion met with acceptance.

There wasn't a response at first.

"Why would I want to make this torture last even longer?" Vicki said finally.

"I was just thinking you might be able to forget about it for a little while. We could eat first and then go over to your house. If you want us to, Randy and I could stay with you when you open the letter. But only if you want us there."

"I don't know," Vicki said.

"Bring the letter with you to the restaurant, and you can open it there," Randy suggested.

"And if it's a rejection?" Vicki questioned.

"Then you'll have all of us to cheer you up," Sierra said, glancing again in the rearview mirror.

"Is that the way you would have wanted to open your letter?" Vicki asked.

Randy shrugged and met Sierra's gaze in the mirror.

"No," Sierra answered for both of them. "You're right. We should just drop you at your house and let you read it alone. Then you can come over to the restaurant to meet us and tell us the good news—because it has to be good news, Vicki. It has to. Randy and I both received good letters today. Now it's your turn."

"One problem," Vicki said. "We just left my car at work."

"Oh, yeah."

"Then you're stuck with us," Randy said. "All for one and one for—"

Vicki leaned forward and grasped the back of Sierra's

seat. "What letter did you get, Sierra? You already heard about Rancho. Did you receive another scholarship?"

"No, something better."

"Oh," Vicki said, letting go of the seat. From the tone in her voice, she seemed to understand that the letter was from Paul. Sierra had received quite a few letters from Paul over the last several months, and though she didn't always confide in Vicki what the letters said, Vicki had been keeping close track of how often he wrote and what the general tone of the correspondence was.

Vicki's interest had resulted from Sierra's request that Vicki and Amy hold her accountable for her imagination, because at one time Sierra had read more into Paul's letters than he was actually saying. With her friends keeping tabs on the relationship, Sierra's feet would stay tethered to the ground.

"You'll have to tell me about your letter," Vicki said as they pulled into the driveway of her house.

"I definitely will." Sierra set the brake and turned around to flash Vicki a smile full of clues as to how wonderful Paul's news was.

But Vicki didn't seem to notice, and her scowl had returned. "I don't want to go in there. I don't want to read the letter."

"Come on," Randy said. "We'll go with you if you want."

"I'm sure it's an acceptance." Even as Sierra said the words, she realized she didn't have a right to say them. What if Vicki wasn't accepted? Sierra had no power over Vicki's future, any more than she had power over her own.

Sierra suddenly realized they were at a major crossroads in their lives, and the words in Vicki's letter could change their friendship forever. An ominous sense of foreboding came over Sierra once more, causing her to remain silent and wait for her friend to make the next move.

"Okay, okay," Vicki finally said with a huff. "Let's get this over with. I want you both to come with me."

Reaching for her door handle, Sierra thought, *And we both want you to come with us.*

chapter two

*V*ICKI'S FRONT DOOR WAS LOCKED. SHE PULLED A key from her backpack and said, "I forgot that my mom said she was going grocery shopping. I'll have to leave her a note to tell her where we're going."

The three friends moved through the living room and into the kitchen at the back of the house. The afternoon sun poured in on the large, round kitchen table and seemed to spotlight the letter that was propped up against a vase of yellow snapdragons.

"There it is," Sierra said, noticing the letter before Vicki did.

Vicki picked up the envelope and stared at it. "I know this is crazy. It's not that big a deal."

"Yes it is," Randy said. "It's a very big deal. At least I think it is."

Vicki looked at Randy. "It's just that I've never waited for a letter like this before. I've never entered a contest and waited to hear if I'd won. Nothing like that."

"So open it!" Sierra blurted out. Both Randy and Vicki snapped their attention to Sierra as if she had invaded a private moment between them. "I mean, won't you feel better at least knowing?"

Vicki looked at the letter and sighed. "I guess." With that she slid her thumbnail under the flap and carefully opened the envelope, a fourth of an inch at a time.

Sierra was running out of patience. This was almost as bad as watching her older sister, Tawni, open Christmas presents. Tawni treated wrapping paper as if it were more precious than the gift itself and needed to be preserved from tearing or crumpling.

At last the single sheet of Rancho Corona University letterhead emerged. Vicki cautiously unfolded it. Both Sierra and Randy read along with her over her shoulder.

"Oh, brother," Sierra muttered. "All that for a letter like this."

"Well, I didn't know," Vicki said with an edge of irritation in her voice.

"What do they mean?" Randy asked. "What form is that?"

"I have no idea," Vicki said.

"It's one of the forms they send in their application packet," Sierra said. "All they're saying is that it wasn't included when you sent in the rest of your stuff; and before they can process your application, they need the form. Do you know where it is? Maybe we could fill it out right now and mail it on the way to the restaurant."

"I'll check the mailer they used to send all the material. I know right where it is in my room."

A thought flashed through Sierra's mind that it was a good thing she wasn't being asked to find anything of such importance in her room. Sierra and Vicki were opposites when it came to orderliness. They had discussed that in one of their conversations about rooming together at college. Sierra had promised Vicki she could and would adjust to Vicki's standard of neatness. After all, for years Sierra had shared a bedroom with tidiness freak Tawni, and Sierra knew how to keep up with Tawni's side of the room when she wanted to—which wasn't often.

Vicki had taken offense that Sierra had compared her to Tawni and insinuated that Vicki was also a tidiness freak. Sierra had changed the subject and silently vowed never again to compare Vicki to Tawni, although their similarities were stronger than she had realized before.

"No news is good news, right?" Sierra said brightly to Randy after Vicki headed down the hallway to her bedroom. "I mean, this isn't so bad. We can go celebrate, and Vicki will be fine."

"I don't know. I think this would be worse than bad news. This only means she has to wait longer to find out. The waiting can be more torturous than a rejection." Randy skimmed the letter one more time.

"Don't you think she'll be accepted, Randy? I mean, it's not that hard to get in."

Randy took off his baseball cap, scratched a spot on the top of his head where his short, blond hair stuck straight up, and then put his cap back on. With his voice lowered, he said, "It's not exactly the same for her as it is for you and me. Vicki doesn't have the grades you have, and she doesn't have the financial need I do. It might be harder for her to get in than we know."

Sierra plucked one of the snapdragons from a stalk in the vase on the kitchen table and pinched the sides gently, making the "dragon" open and close its mouth. "She'll make it. She has to."

"How did you do that?" Randy said, watching Sierra's tiny finger puppet.

"You've never seen a dragon snap before?"

Randy smiled his half smile as Sierra demonstrated again.

"Cool. Let me try."

"Get your own dragon," Sierra said, playfully guarding her fragile pet.

Vicki stepped back into the kitchen with a large manila mailer in her hand.

Randy asked, "Will your mother mind if we play with her flowers?"

"If you do what?" Vicki said.

"Make puppets out of her snapdragons. Do you think she would mind?"

"No. Our backyard is overrun with them."

"Really?" Randy said. "May I pick some?"

Vicki looked up from the papers in her hand. "Are you saying you want to pick some flowers?" She looked confused.

"Yeah. Is that okay?"

"Be my guest," Vicki said, pointing to the back door.

Randy left, and Vicki said, "What's with him? He's in the strangest mood today."

Sierra shrugged and used a squeaky voice to make her tiny flower puppet talk to Vicki. "Maybe he's picking flowers for you as a sign of his undying devotion."

"Oh, right. That's it. I finally wore the right perfume today, and Randy awoke from his coma and noticed me."

Continuing in her high-pitched puppet voice, Sierra said, "Better buy a big bottle of that perfume!"

Vicki glanced at the yellow "mouth" and smiled. "I think he's had too much caffeine today. That's his problem." She went through the papers and pulled out the missing form. "Look. I think this is it. I guess we overlooked it. It has to be signed by my parents, so there's no use spending any more time on it now. I'll leave it here with the letter and let them figure it out."

"Are you bummed?" Sierra asked, returning to her normal voice.

"A little, I guess. It's better than being turned down. But it's not what I was hoping for. Should we get going to the restaurant? I'll leave a note for my mom."

Sierra wondered if Randy was right. Maybe waiting *was* more torturous than having the bad news delivered on the spot. She decided it would help if they got out the door and on to their celebration.

Randy came in the back door but not with an armful of flowers for Vicki, as Sierra had predicted. He had one snapdragon between his fingers, and he was trying to pinch it the way Sierra had. She thought it was funny that he had gone outside to pluck his very own snapdragon. Vicki was right. He was acting strange—or at least stranger than usual.

"Do we need to give Tre a ride?" Sierra asked after

Vicki had finished writing the note telling her parents where she would be.

"I'll call him," Randy said, trying to use a puppet voice and maneuver his snapdragon at the same time.

Vicki motioned for Sierra to follow her into the hallway while Randy made his phone call. Sierra thought of how she had done the same sort of thing so she could tell her mom about Paul's letter. Sierra figured Vicki wanted to hear about the letter, too.

But Paul wasn't the guy on Vicki's mind. "Do you think Randy's acting this way because he heard what you said?"

"What? About the undying devotion?"

Vicki nodded.

"How should I know? Just go with it, girl. Maybe the whole college acceptance letter has rocketed our friend into a more serious approach to his future."

"You think so?" Vicki looked over Sierra's shoulder to see if Randy was coming. She self-consciously smoothed back her long hair.

"Who knows?" Sierra said. "But I can tell you from experience that it's sobering to realize you're about to graduate and go off to college having never dated anyone, much less kissed anyone."

Vicki looked away. "Well, you already know how I feel about that. I wish I were as inexperienced as you are."

Sierra bit her lower lip and tried not to feel a little hurt at Vicki's comment. She knew Vicki meant it in a good way. Yet Sierra still felt bad that she was so inexperienced and had never been kissed. She had been asked out only once, by a guy from school named Drake. Even though she was sure at the time that she was ready for a dating relationship, the experience hadn't turned out well.

Vicki grabbed Sierra's arm and said, "What's wrong?"

"Nothing. Why?"

"Something's bothering you. You're biting your lip."

Sierra immediately ran her tongue across the pinch she had just made on the inside of her lower lip, as if trying to destroy the evidence.

"Ready?" Randy said, joining them from the kitchen. "Tre's going with Margo, and they're leaving his house right now."

"Sure, I'm ready," Vicki said.

"Me, too," Sierra echoed. She leaned closer to Vicki and said, "Nothing's wrong. Really." With a convincing smile, Sierra led her friends to the car and drove them to DiGrassi's Italian restaurant. This time Vicki sat in the front and Randy was alone in the back.

They arrived at the same time as Warner, the band's drummer, did, and the four of them entered the restaurant.

Amy stood at the hostess station. "So what's the big event?"

"Didn't Randy tell you when he called for reservations?" Sierra asked.

Amy shook her head. Her dark bangs brushed her eyelashes as she did.

"We're celebrating!" Sierra told her. "Randy has some news. Tell her, Randy."

Randy shuffled up to the wooden podium with the same enthusiasm with which he had approached Sierra when she was on the porch swing. "I'm going to Rancho

Corona. And there might be a scholarship."

Amy gave Randy a wide smile, which made her dark eyes stand out. "Good for you, Randy. That must be a relief."

Randy nodded. "What about you? Have you made any final decisions?"

Amy shook her head. "I'm still not sure I want to go away to college. Or even if I want to go to college, for that matter."

"You're coming to our graduation, aren't you?" Randy said, stepping closer. Amy had transferred from Royal Academy, the small, private Christian high school that Sierra, Vicki, and Randy attended, to a local public high school whose graduation was a week before Royal Academy's.

"Yes. And you're still coming to mine, aren't you?" She looked at Warner and added, "You're welcome, too, Warner. I'm not having a party or anything, but I was hoping all of you would come to my graduation ceremony."

"We're definitely coming," Randy said.

"You know what?" Vicki added. "We really should have a party, the bunch of us."

The wheels of Sierra's imagination began to turn. She would love to have a party; she could introduce Paul to all of her friends. "Let's!" she said. "I'm sure we can have it at my house."

Just then Tre and Margo came in. They were in the process of becoming a couple lately, and they made an interesting duo. When Tre first came to Royal, he didn't appear to speak much English, although he understood everything. The group later discovered he was quiet because he was shy. Born in Cambodia, he had lived in the Portland area since seventh grade. Tre was the strong, steady backbone of the band. He was the one who always reminded Randy they should pray before practices.

Margo's parents had been missionaries in Peru, where she was born. This was her first year back in the States, and she had gravitated toward Sierra, Randy, and their group. Royal wasn't a big school, and many of the groups were so tightly formed that it was nearly impossible to break into them. Even though they had experienced some difficult moments, the group that had been labeled "Randy and Sierra's circle" had managed to remain open enough that just about anyone could hang out with them.

Lately Margo and Tre had been spending more time together. It seemed they had a lot in common because both of them had grown up in a different culture, and English was their second language. They looked cute, standing next to each other. Both of them had changed into nicer clothes before coming. About a month ago, Margo had colored her short hair a deep brown with red highlights. Sierra thought it looked good, even though Vicki had tried to convince Margo to try lightening it instead.

"How many people are coming?" Amy asked, reaching for the menus and doing a quick head count.

"I think this is it," Randy said. "Did you call anyone else, Tre?"

"Drake and Cassie," Tre answered in his subdued voice. "But they're working on the float for the parade."

Every June, Portland hosted a parade to celebrate the

roses that bloomed abundantly in the rainy City of Roses. Drake's dad owned a diaper delivery service that had participated in the parade every year since the early 1960s. Drake had invited the group to help work on the float, but Sierra had forgotten about the invitation. Or maybe she had wanted to ignore it. She had a decent relationship with Drake, and he really was a nice guy. It was just that he had dated every girl on the planet—or at least every girl at Royal Academy. Sierra was still a little uncomfortable with the thought that last summer she had become one of the many on his list.

"That's right," Randy said. "Maybe we should go over there afterward."

"I have homework," Vicki said a little too quickly.

Sierra decided she would ask Vicki later how she felt about Drake and Cassie being together, since Cassie and Vicki had never gotten along. Whereas Sierra was a little uncomfortable around Drake, Vicki was very uncomfortable around Cassie. It was probably a good thing neither of them had come.

"I'll put you guys in one of the big booths in the back," Amy said, leading the group through the sparsely filled restaurant.

Warner walked beside Sierra. Any attention from him, deliberate or not, made Sierra feel queasy. She was okay with his being around all the time because enough people were in their group that he usually kept his distance from Sierra. The two of them had never found a way to be more than civil to each other. He was one of those people who just got on her nerves, even though she did have to admit he seemed to be trying harder to get along with everyone.

"So you and Randy are both going to Rancho Corona," Warner said. He was much taller than Sierra, and she could almost feel his words pelting the top of her head.

"Yes," she said without looking up at him.

"Who else is going for sure?"

"Vicki," Sierra said confidently.

"I haven't heard yet," Vicki said, turning around and taking in Warner and Sierra in one sweeping glance, "so I'm not a for-sure."

They all slid into the booth, and Sierra sat next to Randy but not near long-legged Warner, who always bumped her legs whenever he sat near her at the school lunch tables. Margo sat next to Sierra, with Tre on the other side. The nice part of the arrangement, in Sierra's opinion, was that Randy was at the center of the booth, which is where he should be for the celebration.

When everyone was nearly finished with dinner, Sierra tapped her spoon against the side of her water glass. "As you all know," she began in her best dinner-hostess voice, "our very own Randy Jenkins has received an important letter today. So we are gathered to celebrate his good news and congratulate him."

Warner lifted his water glass and, in a voice too loud for the quiet restaurant, said, "To Randy!"

The others followed Warner's lead and clinked their glasses in a toast to Randy.

Sierra smiled at her buddy and said, "And now I think the guest of honor should say a few words."

Randy shrugged. "I'm going to college."

"And how do you feel about this big adventure?" Sierra used her spoon as a pretend microphone and held it in front of Randy.

He smiled his half smile and said, "It's a day my mom said she thought would never come."

The group let out a quick burst of laughter.

Sierra cheerfully added, "Yep, only a few short months, and we're outta here!"

An awkward silence fell over the group. Reality was setting in.

Tre was the one who finally spoke for them all. "That's the end of our band."

chapter three

"**Y**OU GUYS STILL HAVE THIS SUMMER," **MARGO** said, leaning forward in the booth. "You have two more bookings at The Beet, and I'm sure some others will come up."

"Just when we were getting pretty good," Warner said.

Again silence came over the small group. To Sierra it felt like the time she had stayed in her seat at the end of a movie she had particularly loved. All the fast action and bright images were replaced with a long list of names on a black screen, and yet she had sat there, absorbing the soft violin music and waiting for all the names to run to the very end. Not until she saw the rectangular logo that said "Dolby Sound" did she really believe the endearing movie was over.

Their senior year wasn't over yet. And this celebration dinner wasn't over, either.

"Anyone save room for dessert?" their waiter asked, stepping up and clearing some of the empty plates.

"Yes!" Sierra answered for them. "And would you ask Amy if she would come over to our table?"

"Certainly. Would you like to see the dessert tray?"

"I already know I want the tiramisù," Sierra said. "And don't you have some kind of cherry tea?"

"Yes, cherry almond. I'll bring you a pot of hot tea. Anyone else?"

The rest of the group placed their dessert orders, and a few minutes later Amy appeared at the table.

"When do you have your break?" Sierra asked.

"I don't know if I get one tonight. I'm here for only a couple of hours."

"Could you see if you could get just a three-minute break? I was hoping you could pull up a chair and have dessert with us."

"I'll ask," Amy said. "It's really slow tonight."

The desserts arrived, and so did Amy with a chair. "I have five minutes," she said, "so everybody talk fast. What's the plan for our graduation party?"

Sierra waited for someone to say something and then remembered she had offered her house. "We haven't decided anything yet," she said. "What do you have in mind?"

Amy's dark eyes lit up. "You know what I've always wanted to do?"

None of them ventured a guess.

"I've always wanted to make a fancy dinner. My uncle said he could get us the lobsters and anything else we needed."

Sierra remembered all too well how she and Amy had planned every detail of a lobster dinner a year ago. They were going to serve the feast to Sierra's older brother

Wesley and to Drake. When their dating lives didn't mate-
rialize as they'd hoped, their dinner plans had dissolved.

"Sounds good to me," Randy said.

"That would be fun," Vicki agreed.

"What if I don't like lobster?" Warner said. "Can we
have something else, too? Like lasagna?"

"You don't like lobster?" Amy said.

"I don't know. I've never had it. But I know I like
lasagna." Warner reminded Sierra of an oversized, spoiled
kid.

"You'll like lobster," Amy promised. "We'll make it with
drawn butter, and you'll love it."

"So, when are we going to have the party?" Margo
asked. "The same day as graduation?"

"My family has a bunch of company coming for my
graduation," Vicki said. "What if we did it the night before?
Sort of a pre-graduation party just for us?"

"Are you guys going on the senior getaway next weekend?" Margo asked. "I heard that not many people signed
up."

"I signed up," Vicki said. "But when I found out it was
$350 for only two nights on the coast, I took my name off
the list. I have no idea why they made it so expensive. I
sure can't afford that. And with all the other graduation
expenses, my parents couldn't afford it, either."

Warner gave a full report on the senior getaway plans.
A group of parents had organized a weekend on the Ore-
gon coast for the seniors, since Royal Academy didn't have
a prom or senior dinner or anything like the other schools
in town. The parents had reserved two floors of rooms at

a hotel on the beach. They had made it clear the guys would be on one floor and the girls on another. There would be sufficient chaperons and only two students per room. Lights-out would be at midnight. The well-meaning organizers had listed more rules on their flyer than they had listed benefits. And the highlights were supposed to be the aquarium and miniature golfing—not exactly activities at the top of the seniors' list of ways to celebrate a milestone in their lives—especially not for that price.

"I think that whole senior getaway is going to crash. Nobody has the money to go," Vicki said.

"Didn't we have to sign up by last Friday?" Sierra said. "I don't know anyone who's going."

"Then we'll do our own party," Margo said. "I think a dinner is a great idea." She flashed a smile at Tre, and Sierra wondered if this was going to turn into a date event. Sierra quickly did the math. Three "natural" matched-up couples were at the table right now. The only unmatched ones were Sierra and Warner. Her skin began to feel clammy at the thought. Then she remembered Paul was coming and laughed aloud.

"What?" Amy asked.

"Nothing. Nothing. Let's plan the party. Whatever you guys want is fine with me, as long as it's after the 12th."

"I have to get back to work," Amy said. "I'll call you later tonight, Sierra, and we can plan everything, okay?"

"Great," Sierra said. Her heart was soaring at the thought of Paul's being at a fancy dinner and fun party with her friends. He would love them, and they would love him. The thought was even more fanciful because her mom was the only one who knew about Paul's coming. It was kind of sweet to have a secret with just her mom.

Never being great at keeping secrets, Sierra told Vicki her news on their way back to the dealership. Randy had gotten a ride with Tre and Margo because they were going to check on Drake and the parade preparations. As soon as Sierra had Vicki in the car, she told her what Paul had said in his letter.

Vicki squealed and grabbed Sierra's arm in her excitement for her friend. "I can't believe you didn't tell me right away!"

"So much happened so fast."

"That is really great news, Sierra! I'm so happy for you. What else did he say?"

"I don't know. I didn't even finish reading the letter. I only read the first few paragraphs. Then Randy showed up, and his news superseded my news. Then we went to pick you up, and we were all wondering about your letter—"

"My letter," Vicki said, interrupting Sierra and suddenly sobering. "It's awful not to know if I'm going to Rancho now that Randy has been accepted. And you, too. I thought about it at dinner when Tre was talking about the band breaking up. I got really depressed. We need to make our graduation party something special, as Amy was saying."

"I agree," Sierra said.

"And you know what else I realized at dinner?" Vicki said. "Our Monday afternoons at Mama Bear's are going to be over, too."

For several months now, Sierra, Amy, and Vicki had met every Monday afternoon at 4:00 at Mama Bear's

Bakery for what Amy called "soul cleansing." Sierra thought Amy's term was a little too cosmic for what they talked about. To Sierra, Monday afternoons with her two friends meant an uninterrupted time of deep, honest conversation in a quiet corner with a pot of tea and a shared cinnamon roll. Amy, Vicki, and Sierra hadn't always been on peaceful terms. So when the three of them forged this unlikely friendship triangle, they all felt a common desire to do whatever it took to hold on to the fragile bonds.

When they had visited colleges in the spring, Amy had made it clear she didn't want to attend a Christian school. That was because ever since her parents had divorced last fall, she had questioned her beliefs in God and the church. Why would she want to go to a place that taught stuff she wasn't sure was right?

Sierra thought Amy's problem was that she held too much inside. Even though she called their time a "soul cleansing," she was the one who opened up the least. She listened, though—and asked questions. Vicki and Sierra had learned over the past few months that love is patient, especially when a friend is hurting and needs someone to be there, someone who genuinely loves her and isn't bent on forcing change before she is ready.

Often the Monday afternoons had been the highlight of Sierra's week—especially during the weeks she didn't receive a letter from Paul. She had two friends who would listen to her talk at length about whatever was on her mind, and Sierra had learned she could trust Vicki and Amy to keep confidences. If it was a soul cleansing for Amy, their time together was a fragrant sanctuary for Sierra.

"You know what I'll miss the most?" Vicki said as Sierra came to a stoplight. "I'll miss the way I always feel when I wake up on Monday mornings. I used to hate to get up. Then, when we started to meet, I'd hop out of bed and think about what to wear and how the day couldn't go fast enough before we could get together."

Sierra smiled. The light changed, and she pulled into the intersection and began to make a left turn, sanctioned by the green arrow overhead. The terrible sound of squealing brakes came barreling toward them, and Vicki screamed. A pickup truck swerved to miss Sierra's car and stopped dead center in the intersection. All the other cars shrieked to a halt. Miraculously, no one was hit.

It appeared the driver of the pickup had decided to run the yellow light and then had changed his mind at the last minute but couldn't stop his vehicle. Everyone sat frozen in their cars, looking at each other. The pickup backed up slowly. The guy in the car behind Sierra honked his horn. The turn signal was now yellow, so she quickly put the car in gear and motored through the mess and onto the street that led to the dealership.

"Look at me," Vicki said, holding out her hand. "I'm shaking. How can you be so calm? We could have been killed, Sierra. A few more feet and that pickup would have smashed us."

"I know," Sierra said quietly. She drove with extra caution to the dealership and pulled into the side area where Vicki's car was still parked. Then Sierra turned off the engine, and the two sobered friends sat silently for a few minutes.

"How do people make it through life if they don't know for sure they're going to heaven when they die?" Vicki asked. She turned in her seat and faced Sierra. "I mean, stuff like that happens to everyone, doesn't it? Near brushes with disaster and split seconds where only a few feet mean the difference between life and death."

Sierra nodded, still shaken inside.

"If I didn't know for sure I was saved and that the instant I die I'll be in heaven, I think an experience like we just had would completely terrify me. I'd be traumatized for life."

"I know," Sierra said. "It's moments like this that I get this sick feeling inside when I think about friends like Amy who say they're uninterested in settling their relationships with God."

Vicki and Sierra exchanged glances of painful agreement.

"Let's talk to her on Monday," Vicki said. "We can say it in a way that she'll listen to us. I know we can."

Sierra agreed.

After making sure Vicki got safely into her house, Sierra cautiously drove home. Amy called about 10 minutes after Sierra was in her room. Sierra's dad brought the cordless phone to her and asked her to return it downstairs when she was finished with her conversation because the batteries were running low.

"Amy?" Sierra said.

"Hi. I asked my uncle about the lobsters, and he said he would give me a price on them tomorrow. I thought if everyone chipped in, it wouldn't be so much. For the salad and dessert, I asked him if we could buy them from the restaurant, too. Then all we would have to do is boil the lobsters and get some bread and maybe a vegetable. What do you think?"

Sierra moved some clothes and papers from the over-stuffed chair by her open window and said, "Sounds great. I haven't talked to my parents yet. Why don't I call you back after I ask them? How many people do you think we'll have?"

"Around 10 to 12 is what I told my uncle."

"Guess who one of those 10 to 12 will be," Sierra said, smiling mischievously into the receiver.

"Wes?" Amy guessed.

"No; guess again."

"I don't know."

"It's someone you would never guess."

"Not Nathan!" Amy said in a panic. "Randy wouldn't invite him, would he? I know they've become good friends from The Beet, but Randy knows how awkward that would be for me, doesn't he?"

"Don't worry," Sierra said, assuring Amy that her old boyfriend wouldn't be on the guest list. "It's not Nathan. But it is a guy."

Amy sounded frustrated as she said, "Come on, Sierra, just tell me."

Sierra smiled and said the one name that was often on her lips in silent prayer. The name of the guy who had written to her for almost a year. The name she thought about daily but rarely spoke aloud. "Paul."

chapter four

"*P*AUL?" AMY REPEATED. "HE'S COMING TO YOUR graduation?"

"Yes. I just received the letter today. He arrives on the 12th, and he'll be here for four days."

"Oh, Sierra, you must be in heaven!"

Amy's choice of words struck an all-too-recent memory, and Sierra abruptly changed topics in response to the knot she felt in her stomach. "I want to ask you something, Amy, and I don't want you to get upset."

"Okay. Sure." Amy could change her moods faster than anyone Sierra had ever known. At the moment Amy was in a good mood, which was why Sierra forged ahead.

"When I was taking Vicki home, we were nearly hit by a pickup truck. It made us both start thinking about dying and how we know we're going to heaven. And, Amy, I know we agreed not to talk about this stuff with you, but I have to tell you, it really scared me to think you might not know you're going to heaven because you say you're undecided about God."

Silence was the only response on the other end of the line.

"Amy, don't be mad. And don't hang up. I just had to say that because I really, really care. Amy, I love you, and I don't want you to go to hell."

A thunderous "Click!" sounded in Sierra's ear, followed by the lonely whine of the dial tone.

What have I done? Sierra dropped her head into her hands and reviewed her last few sentences. *Why did I say it that way? Why didn't I wait until Monday, as Vicki suggested, and let Vicki do the talking? Why, oh why do I blast out my thoughts and feelings like that?*

Before Sierra could thoroughly beat herself up, the phone rang in her lap. She grabbed it, pushed the button, and answered with, "I'm sorry. I shouldn't have said it that way."

The party on the other end didn't respond. Then it dawned on Sierra that the caller might be someone other than Amy.

"Amy?" she ventured.

"Sierra?" the male voice answered.

"Yes."

Deep laughter came to her over the receiver. She had no idea who was on the other end. "I take it you and Amy are having another go-round."

"Something like that," Sierra said cautiously, trying to place the voice and wondering why he said "go-round."

"How are things for you, other than with Amy?"

"Pretty good," she said slowly. "And with you?" She was hoping for a clue of any kind.

The phone line began to crackle, and the guy's answer was muffled and sounded too far away for Sierra to decipher.

Oh no, the batteries are going! Sierra thought in a panic. "Can you call back?" she shouted into the phone. "If you can hear me, I'm going to hang up, and you'll need to call back because this phone is going dead."

Suddenly, his voice was clear and loud once more. "Are you there?"

"Yes, but I have to get to a different phone. The batteries are going dead on this one. Can you just call back?"

"Sure."

The phone line began to crackle again, and Sierra hung up. She headed downstairs, wondering who this caller could be. Then the realization struck her with such a "boom" that she screamed as she thudded down the last four stairs and skidded on the hardwood floor of the entryway in her stocking feet.

Mr. Jensen came running from the living room with the remote-control switch in his hand. "What is it?"

Sierra held out the dead phone. "It's Paul! He just called, and I hung up on him."

Mrs. Jensen appeared from the living room, too, and said, "He'll call back, won't he?"

The phone rang again, and Sierra pushed the button, but the phone kept ringing. Mr. Jensen took off for the phone in the den, and Sierra followed, hot on his heels. "Don't you dare!" she called out to her dad.

He grabbed the phone before Sierra could pull it from his grasp. Sierra's dad had many fine qualities, but he had one serious, incurable flaw. He harassed any guy who called for his daughters. Now that Tawni had moved out, Mr. Jensen had doubled his teasing of Sierra's guy friends. Poor Paul! He was calling from Scotland and wouldn't understand her dad's demented hobby. Paul might be the one to hang up this time.

"Is this Paul?" Sierra heard her dad say when he answered the phone. She tried to pry the phone from his ear, but he was using both hands to hold it firmly in place.

"This is Mr. Jensen, Paul. I'd like to know exactly what your intentions are toward my daughter."

"Daddy!" Sierra gritted out through clenched teeth. "Don't do this! Can't you just take up golf like a normal father?"

Her dad's eyebrows raised in seeming approval as he listened to Paul's answer. "In that case, I'll let you talk directly to her. That is, if she still wants to talk to you."

Sierra put one hand on her hip and held out her other hand to receive the phone.

"Or, actually," Mr. Jensen went on, dragging out the agonizing seconds for Sierra, "I should say, if you still want to talk to her. She dyed her hair blue yesterday and had all her teeth pulled. But the rash on her face is beginning to clear up."

"Dad!"

He laughed at whatever Paul's comment was. "Here she is. You take care, Paul. Pleasure talking with you."

Mr. Jensen offered Sierra the phone. She put her hand over the receiver and waited for him to close the door behind him as he left.

"Hi," she said, trying to sound calm. "I'd apologize for my dad, but there's no excuse for him when he gets like that."

"I told him you looked good in blue, so the hair shouldn't be a problem."

Sierra laughed.

"It's good to hear your laugh, little Daffodil Queen," Paul said, his voice sounding clear and as close as if he were standing right beside her. Sierra closed her eyes and let his tender nickname for her melt into her heart.

"It's really good to hear your voice," Sierra echoed. She felt as if she might start to cry and pursed her lips together. Poor Paul had already paid for two phone calls and had endured an interview with her dad. The last thing he needed was to listen to her blubbering for sheer joy. "I got your letter today," she said, forcing herself to be even-keeled.

"Good. So you know I was able to make arrangements to come on the 12th. Is it okay with you if I come to your graduation?"

"Yes, of course. I'd love to have you come. My friends and I are planning a party. Maybe a dinner. It will probably be here at my house. I'm so glad you're coming."

"Now, you are being honest with me, aren't you? I'm not crashing your party or any other plans with your friends?"

"No, not at all! Having you here will be the best part of my whole graduation."

Paul hesitated.

Sierra bit her lower lip, wondering if she had said too

much. Had she sounded too eager? Too forceful? From the beginning, Paul had let her know that he wanted to take their relationship nice and slow. Never once had he signed his letters with the word "Love." Never once had he written anything that indicated they were more than friends. Sierra was the one who kept running ahead, assuming and making more of the relationship than was actually there. She had tried so hard to pull back, go slowly, and be realistic. Had she ruined everything now?

"You know what?" Paul replied slowly. "Seeing you again will be the best part of my trip home."

Sierra's heart soared. This wasn't the kind of response she expected to hear from Paul. Suddenly, she felt shy, which was out of character for her. Her mind raced with all the possibilities. What was he thinking? Was he ready to move forward in their relationship?

"I have a lot of things I'm eager to talk to you about, Sierra," Paul continued. "It will be great to finally see you again and say those things face-to-face."

"Uh-huh" was the only sound that came from Sierra's lips. She chided herself and scrambled to find something more intelligent to say.

Paul went on. "Remember that café we went to last year?"

"Yes; Carla's." Sierra spilled out the words quickly. "Of course I remember."

"Good. I'm hoping you remember how to get there. I thought it would be nice to stop in for a mug of good Northwest coffee. I know this is pathetic, but I've even had dreams about mocha lattes like I used to get at a little drive-through place. I seem to remember Carla's Café had pretty good coffee, too."

"Oh," Sierra said. Another brilliant response. She couldn't help but feel her emotions plummet when he said he had been dreaming about coffee at Carla's. Sierra had dreams about the same place, only in *her* dreams she and Paul were at the same table by the window where they had sat a year ago. This time, instead of his teasing her because he had heard she had a crush on him, Paul was holding her hand and confessing his love for her.

"What did you think of the rest of my letter?" Paul asked.

"To tell you the truth—" Sierra began.

She was going to confess to not having had a chance to read the rest of his letter, but Paul interrupted her and said, "Of course you'll tell me the truth. That's what you do best. You're a proclaimer, Sierra. You proclaim the truth. That's one of the things I wanted to tell you face-to-face, but I guess I'll say it now. I know I've given you a hard time in the past about being zealous. Lately I've come to appreciate that quality in you, and I wanted to tell you."

"Thanks." All Sierra could think at the moment was how her truth speaking might have just "proclaimed" Amy out of her life for good. But all she said to Paul was, "I appreciate your encouragement."

"I'm the one who appreciates your encouragement," Paul said. "Your letters have meant so much to me this year. So have all the verses you sent me, and all the prayers I know you've prayed for me. You'll never know what a difference you've made in my life. I'm serious, Sierra. I really think God used you in a big way to turn my life around, and that's why I wrote the poem for you that I put at the end of the letter. It's the first poem I've written just for you."

He paused again. All she could say was, "Thanks, Paul." It would be too awkward to mention she hadn't read the whole letter now.

"I was going to wait and read it to you when I saw you, but I decided to go ahead and send it. Some things are easier to say on paper than in person."

"That's true," Sierra said.

"Well, I guess I'd better hang up or I won't have enough money left to buy either of us a cup of coffee by the time we get to Carla's."

Sierra quickly tried to think of what she should ask him before he hung up. "Do you need a ride from the airport?"

"No, Uncle Mac is picking me up."

"What time do you get in?"

"Around 10:00."

"In the morning on the 12th?" Sierra asked hopefully.

"No, 10:00 at night."

"Well, I'm just glad you're coming. It will be so good to see you again and finally talk in person." Sierra tried hard to contain her feelings. She wanted to blurt out crazy words like, "I love you, Paul MacKenzie! I can't wait to throw my arms around you and smell that pine-tree fresh aftershave you wear."

Fortunately for both of them, she kept her wild thoughts to herself.

"I'll give you a call from the Highland House when I get in. Or maybe it'll be the morning of the 13th if I arrive too late. It's less than a week and a half away."

"I know," Sierra said in a voice that revealed her eager heart. "I'll be counting the days."

After a tiny pause, Paul said just before hanging up, "So will I, Daffodil Queen."

chapter five

*S*IERRA FELT AS IF ALL THE AIR HAD BEEN SUCKED FROM the room when she heard the click on Paul's end of the line. She was still standing in the middle of the den where she had taken the phone from her dad. The whole time she and Paul had talked, Sierra hadn't moved. She hadn't even thought of sitting down. It was as if she had been suspended in time and space. Maybe if she closed her eyes tightly enough, Paul's voice would come back over the dead line of the phone she still held to her ear. But the only sound she heard was the wail of the dial tone.

As though pulling herself out of a deep dream and back to the dawn of a new day, Sierra opened her eyes slowly and forced herself to return the phone to its cradle. She wanted to remember every word, every nuance.

The poem! My poem! She hurried from the den and grabbed her backpack from the coat tree in the entryway.

"Is everything all set with Paul's trip?" Mrs. Jensen asked, stepping into the entryway.

"Yes. He'll be here the night of the 12th, after 10:00." Sierra reached into the backpack and pulled out Paul's letter. "So that ruins our plans for the dinner party."

"Our plans for the dinner party?" Mrs. Jensen questioned.

"Oh. I didn't talk to you about it yet. We were all talking about having a dinner party for graduation. Amy said she could get lobsters." As soon as she mentioned Amy, Sierra remembered the way her friend had hung up on her 20 minutes ago. She needed to call Amy back. And she needed to talk over the dinner party plans with her mom. But all she wanted to do was flee to her room, where she could read Paul's letter and take into her heart the poem he had written for her alone.

"And you wanted to have the party here?" Mrs. Jensen asked.

"Yes, if that's okay. But now I don't know when to have it. We thought the day before graduation, but Paul won't be here in time, and I really want him at the party."

"It could be just as special with your friends and without Paul," Mrs. Jensen said.

An image flashed into Sierra's mind of her being paired with Warner, and she said, "No, believe me, Mom, it won't be the same. I only want to have it when Paul's here."

They stood in the hallway, discussing options, but none seemed to work.

Mr. Jensen, who could hear them talking from the living room, called out, "Why don't you have it the night of graduation? We can have the family over the night before. Then they can go home right after graduation, and you can have your friends over. Isn't the ceremony at 2:00? That'll give you plenty of time for a fancy dinner."

"What about the other kids, Howard? Don't you suppose they might have family parties on graduation day?"

"Amy isn't," Sierra said. "Her graduation is this weekend. And Randy hasn't said anything about a lot of company. I don't know about Vicki."

"I suppose it's worth a try," Mrs. Jensen said. "Let me know as soon as you find out, and I'll make the calls to our family."

Sierra went back to the den and took the letter with her. Eventually she would get to it, but first she had some calls to make. Sierra dialed Amy's number and waited for her to pick it up, not exactly sure what to say. On the sixth ring, Amy answered.

"It's me. I'm sorry. Can we talk?"

"Why do you do this, Sierra? Things are going nice and smooth in our friendship, and then you have to say something that puts us both on edge."

"I'm not sorry for what I said, just the way I said it. I could have said it a lot better."

"Oh, really?"

"Can we talk about something else for a minute? It's the dinner party at my house. Paul doesn't get in until late on the night of the 12th. My dad suggested we have the party on Friday night, after the graduation ceremony, which is at 2:00. What do you think?"

"I think it's amazing the way you can switch moods so fast."

"Me switch moods? You're the one who switches moods all the time, Amy."

"But I don't go around telling you you're going to hell

and then call back and say, 'By the way, can you bring the lobsters over Friday?' "

Sierra sighed. "Did it really sound like that, Amy? I'm sorry. Can we put the whole heaven and hell topic to the side until our Monday get-together? I want to talk about it more and tell you why I feel strongly about it, but I think it would be better with Vicki there, too."

"Why? So you can gang up on me?"

"No, of course not."

"You and Vicki have no idea what I believe or where I am in my relationship with God."

"Exactly," Sierra said. "And that's why I want to talk about it. I always let you talk about the things that are important to you; now I think it's only fair you let me talk about what's important to me."

Amy paused, then said, "Okay, you're right. We can talk Monday. And yes, I think next Friday would be a good night for the dinner, mostly because I already have the night off."

"Good," Sierra said. "Great, actually. I'm going to call everyone else to see if we can set it up for then."

"Okay. I'll talk to you later."

Sierra called Vicki and Randy and told them the plan. They both said they would try to convince their parents to have their family parties the night before like Sierra's family. Neither of them expected many relatives to come, so it sounded like a good possibility. Randy agreed to call the guys in the band with the same information, and Vicki said she would call Margo and a couple of other girls they were thinking of inviting.

That settled, Sierra eagerly headed for her room, where she could read the rest of Paul's letter without being interrupted. Passing the living room, she stopped in the doorway to watch the end of a funny commercial with her parents. Then she told them the plans were working out. Mrs. Jensen said she would make the arrangements tomorrow and told Sierra to relax about everything.

"This is your graduation, honey. We want you to have a memorable time and enjoy the occasion with both your friends and your family."

On impulse, Sierra dashed over to the couch and gave her mom and dad a big hug. "You guys are the best parents in the world. Did you know that?"

Her startled parents gave each other looks of pleased surprise.

Mr. Jensen said, "Would you mind convincing Gavin of that? He's still upset that we won't let him go to the Burnside Skate Park on Saturday with his friends from school."

"He wants to go there?" Sierra said. "He's too young. Almost all the skaters there are in high school and much more experienced on skateboards than Gavin. They would run over him. Besides, the Rose Parade is this Saturday. Downtown will be jam-packed with people."

"That's right," Mrs. Jensen said. "We should go to the parade—as a family."

"I have to work," Sierra said. "And I can't take time off because Mrs. Kraus already gave me the next weekend off for graduation."

"We still might go," Mrs. Jensen said. "It could be a

nice outing for Granna Mae if the weather is clear."

"I'm going to bed," Sierra said. "Thanks again for adjusting the family plans for me."

"Flexibility is a sign of good mental health," Sierra's dad said.

Sierra looked to her mom for an explanation.

"He's been reading those pamphlets the doctor gave us last week at Granna Mae's checkup."

Sierra nodded her understanding and headed upstairs with Paul's letter in hand. Sierra's grandmother had an undiagnosed condition that had grown worse over the last few years. She was sometimes as normal and clear thinking as ever, but then, without warning, she would blip into another dimension and become lost and confused. Sierra and her family had moved here a year and a half ago to be with Granna Mae in her large Victorian house and to care for her. The Jensen family adored Granna Mae and was understanding and considerate of her difficulties most of the time. But every now and then watching her became exhausting, especially for Sierra's mom, who had to do most of the overseeing.

Alone in the cluttered haven of her beloved bedroom, Sierra went directly to the overstuffed chair by the window. She pulled back the sheer curtains and pushed the chipped wooden window frame all the way up. She had to use a board to keep it open. The soothing night breezes invited themselves in, ruffling the sheers. Two birds in the huge cedar tree began a happy concert of night songs. The sky, painted a hazy periwinkle blue in the late dusk, showed off its prized jewel, a crescent-shaped ivory moon hanging above the cedar tree.

Sierra drew in a deep breath, filling her lungs with the sweet fragrance of late spring and filling her heart with a prayer of thankfulness to God for all the beauty He had placed in her life. If she was grateful to her earthly parents for their love and understanding, she was even more grateful to her heavenly Father for His lovingkindness to her.

Feeling like celebrating, Sierra lit a candle she had received as a birthday present from Vicki months ago. Since Vicki knew Sierra liked daffodils, the candle was in the shape of a bright yellow daffodil blossom. It rested on a saucer with the trumpet part of the flower facing up and the wick in the middle of the trumpet.

Sierra placed the lit daffodil candle on her dresser. Gazing at her reflection in the mirror, she fussed a little with her unruly hair. She rummaged for some lip gloss and applied it to the cracked skin on the right corner of her mouth. Then she whispered another prayer of thanks to God for protecting her and Vicki from the near-collision with the pickup.

Since the night was still young, Sierra decided to treat herself to something she had done only a few times because it took so long. She decided she would read Paul's letter and then go back and read all the letters he had ever written to her. She kept them in the large bottom drawer of her dresser in an old hatbox she had found at Christmastime in the attic. Her dad had sent her there in search of more Christmas lights, and when she had found the old silver and gray box, she had fallen in love with it. A handful of yellowed tissue paper was stuffed into the box, but the hat Granna Mae had once stored there was long gone.

Pulling open the bottom drawer, Sierra extracted the hatbox and settled herself by the window for a long visit with Paul's precious words on a glorious spring evening.

The new letter came first. She skimmed the part she had already read that afternoon about his plans to come on the 12th and then read on.

> As I've been preparing to leave here, I've been surprised at how much my life and my heart have changed since I arrived on a blustery day last June. I guess I blew into Edinburgh with about the same level of cool indifference to God as the storm that came in with me. The seasons changed, and so did I. I actually feel I've lived several lifetimes in the 12 months I've been here. Several seasons, at least.
>
> For the first time in my life, I truly know God. Is that too bold to declare? It's what I feel. He's no longer just all around me or visible in the lives of people like my dad and my grandfather. He is alive in me. My life is no longer mine to control. I'm hidden inside His eternal life, and for as long as I walk this earth, the Good Shepherd will direct me.
>
> You know that image of Christ being the Good Shepherd, don't you? It's in John 10. Lately that chapter has become very real to me, especially the parts, " . . . he calls his own sheep by name," and "I am the door of the sheep. . . . If anyone enters by Me, he will be saved, and will go in and out and find pasture." I've finally entered through that door, and I'm finding pasture, as the verse says.

Scotland has been an easy place to learn about sheep and pastures. I'm more aware than ever how clueless sheep can be. They follow the rest of the flock instead of following the shepherd. More than once I've seen how the failure of a lamb to follow the shepherd's directions has ended in the damage and sometimes destruction of that lamb, especially when the storms come in.

Why am I telling you all this? Because I am a sheep, and for far too long I followed the mindless bleating and frantic scurrying of the other sheep. But I have heard my Shepherd's voice, as He has called me patiently to Himself, and I have come.

God has answered all your prayers, Sierra. There is no turning back for me now. How can I ever thank you for persistently proclaiming the truth to me, even when I didn't want to hear it? How can I tell you how much your prayers have meant to me? You never gave up on me, even when I gave you no reason to keep praying. You are one of His sheep, Sierra—a very special one. Your heart is wise beyond your years. You stood by what you believed and boldly proclaimed the truth. Thank you.

Sierra stopped reading only long enough to bounce up for a tissue. Her tears were dripping on the letter, causing the black ink to smear slightly. She couldn't believe Paul was saying all these things to her. In his previous letters, he had never been this transparent.

Blowing her nose and tossing the tissue onto the floor, Sierra read on. Two more onionskin pages of Paul's bold writing remained for her to take into her heart.

chapter six

S IERRA CONTINUED TO READ PAUL'S LETTER AT THE top of the next page.

I've done a lot of thinking and praying about what the Shepherd wants me to do when I leave here. The first thing I believe He wants me to do is apologize to some people in Portland from school last year. I also want to tell them what God has done and how He's changed me. That's part of the reason I wanted to come to Portland before going home.

I also need to have a serious talk with my parents to set a few things right there. It sure is easier to mess things up than to put them back in order. I considered writing my parents or calling them but then decided it would be best if I talked to them in person. I need to ask their forgiveness for a couple of things, too.

I know God has forgiven me for the past, but He wasn't the only one I wronged, so I need to do whatever I can to make it right with several people. Please pray for me about this. It's not going to be easy, but I know that's the next step.

I've made a serious commitment to the Lord regarding the future, and I believe He's invited me to go into the ministry in some form or other. I don't know if it's to be a pastor, a missionary, a full-time Christian service worker like my uncle Mac, or what. All I know is that this is the next step for me, and I'm excited about moving forward. So please pray for me as you've never prayed before!

Before I close, I wanted to send you this poem. I wrote it for you, Sierra, after a hike I took in the Highlands a few weeks ago. As I opened the gate at the end of the trail and walked through the pasture, I knew it would probably be my last hike in these hills I've come to love.

You should have seen all the new spring lambs. They were so small, huddled next to the ewes. The sight reminded me of how small I felt and how eager I was to stay close to Jesus, my Good Shepherd. It had only been two days since God and I had talked everything out and I had sensed His calling me into the ministry. Perhaps someday I'll tell you how that all happened.

But what prompted this poem was a sight I'll never forget. Past the meadow, as I climbed higher, I came to a rocky area that was covered with wild heather. I don't care much for heather. It's prickly to the touch, and the colors are so pale. There, in the middle of all this heather, next to a gray rock, stood one brilliant yellow daffodil, lifting its trumpet to the heavens. I stopped, amazed at how that single daffodil could change the dreariness of an entire hillside.

That's when I thought of you, Daffodil Queen. You

stand out just like that brilliant yellow flower, defying
all that is common. Your words are like the bold blasting
of a trumpet across a world of pale, prickly lives. And
you know what? I said it the day I met you, and I'll say
it again: Don't ever change, Sierra.

                              With affection,
                                 Paul

Sierra had to reach for the tissues again before she
could read the poem. Her eyes were blurring, her nose was
dripping, and her heart was melting.

Taking a deep breath, she glanced at the flickering light
of the daffodil candle on her dresser and wished with all
her heart she had read Paul's letter before he had called.
She would have said ever so much more to him.

And he had signed the letter, "With affection." He had
never written that before.

Tossing two more used tissues onto the floor, Sierra
reached over and turned on the lamp beside the chair. It
had grown dark outside. The birds had subdued their concert, and the streetlight was now competing with the
moonlight. Sierra had never felt like this before in her life.
No one had ever said words to her like Paul just had. No
one had ever made her believe she was okay just the way
she was—better than okay: She was special, unique, and
appreciated.

" 'With affection,' " she repeated. "That is so perfect."

Sierra held the last page with the poem in her lap. She
almost didn't want to read it. *What if I don't like it? What*
if it's really, really mushy? Am I ready to let my feelings for

Paul out of the prison I've held them captive in for so long?
My life is much less complicated when I don't let my emotions
run wild and cause all kinds of destruction. What happens
once they're let loose?

Then she realized she was already a changed woman.
Just the few affectionate lines Paul had written were enough
to alter her opinion of herself. Those words were etched
in her memory. She had to read the poem. She had to
devour every word Paul had written, especially when those
words were a poem written for her alone.

The title was simply "Daffodil."

> *Bold you stand beside your Rock*
> *Proclaiming Truth;*
> *Eternal, unchanging,*
> *To a thorny crowd,*
> *Resistant, proud*
> *Who mock your words.*
> *Still you stand firm beside the Rock*
> *Trumpeting Truth;*
> *You fearless, Golden Daffodil.*
> *One from the crowd,*
> *Resistant, proud,*
> *Took your words*
> *Into his heart*
> *And never*
> *Will he be the same.*
> *So stand bold and firm,*
> *Sweet Daffodil.*
> *Surprise the world as only you can.*

Sierra reread the poem, taking in Paul's words and noting that he called her "Sweet Daffodil." A P.S. was added at the bottom of the page:

> *I should tell you that the morning before I took that inspirational walk I had been reading in Philippians. Read chapter 1, verses 19–21 when you have a chance. It reminded me of you. I wrote those verses out on a card that I now carry in my wallet. I guess you could say I've taken them on as my life verses. See you soon.*
>   *Paul*

Sierra leaned back in the chair and looked out the window into the soft June night. For a long time she just sat there, staring, with Paul's letter in her lap. All his past letters went unread. In 10 days she would look into Paul's blue-gray eyes and hear his deep voice. Would he take her in his arms and draw her close to his heart in a tight hug? What would he think when he saw her? She had changed a lot in the year since they had last seen each other. At least, she thought she had changed. It made her realize how young and inexperienced she had been when she first met him.

The memory brought a smile to her lips. They had met at a phone booth—not just any phone booth, but one at the Heathrow Airport in London. She was waiting to use the phone, and Paul had borrowed some change from her to complete his call.

How funny! Sierra thought. *He was calling his old girlfriend. I actually gave him money to call Jalene! Hey, I don't*

think he ever paid me back. I'll have to remind him when I
see him . . . in only 10 days.

Sierra was still floating through her private dreamland
the next day at school. It seemed pointless to even attend
classes, since the teachers had "senioritis" even worse than
the students did. In her first class they watched a video;
second period was open study for the final on Thursday;
and since the weather was nice, her fourth-period teacher
took them outside and let everyone sit around and talk.

By the end of the day, Sierra had accomplished nothing.
She had learned nothing new. She hadn't studied a pinch.
But she had crafted wonderfully sweet plans for the few
days she and Paul would have together. In addition to the
lobster dinner and graduation ceremony, her mental list
included a picnic at Multnomah Falls; a dinner cruise on
the Willamette River; an afternoon browsing through
books together at Powell's Bookstore downtown; a video
night at home with the family, eating Mrs. Jensen's famous
caramel corn; a hike up to Pittock Mansion in the West
Portland Hills; and maybe a concert or play, depending on
what was available downtown. If nothing there interested
them, they could always tour the art museums. And of
course they would go to Carla's Café at least once.

Sierra continued to spin her plans as the week went
on. She made a list and checked into each activity, calling
for show times, prices on dinner cruises, and hours when
Powell's was open. The list turned into a notebook of
collected information. She even picked up a few brochures
at a restaurant that advertised other activities she hadn't
thought of, such as the antique stores in Sellwood and a

visit to Haystack Rock on the coast in Cannon Beach. This was a good time of year for windsurfing up in the Columbia Gorge. They could rent jet skis at a landing on the Vancouver side of the Columbia River. And there was also a restored steam engine train up in Battle Ground that they could ride through a park, which might be fun for their picnic day.

Her notebook soon turned into an organized, detailed travel portfolio of the Portland area. If only Sierra could have turned it in for a grade, she would have loved to accept that grade for one of her finals.

As it was, she barely received an A- on one and two Bs on the others. It was one of the first times in her high school career that she had received anything below an A on a final. When one of her teachers questioned her, Sierra answered that the motivation wasn't there. She had worked for so many years to have good enough grades to make it into any college she wanted, and now she had been accepted at Rancho Corona, had three academic scholarships, and it was the very end of school. What she didn't tell her teacher was that her mind couldn't hold another scholastic detail because it was too full of important information—information such as what time the antique stores in Sellwood closed on Saturday and what movies were playing at what times at the Lloyd Center.

When Sierra, Vicki, and Amy met for their Monday afternoon tea time, Sierra brought her notebook and spread it out on the table, asking her friends' opinions about the two different boats that offered dinner cruises on the Willamette.

Vicki laughed. She didn't seem to be able to stop.

Sierra felt humiliated and indignant. "I don't see why you think this is so funny."

"You tend to do things to the extreme," Vicki said, trying to pull a straight face. "When did you have time to do all this, Sierra? You worked two afternoons last week and all day Saturday, and we were at Amy's graduation on Friday. Plus it was finals week!"

"I had time."

"We always find the time to do the things we love," Amy said, coming to Sierra's defense. "I think it's great. If you wanted to, you could sell this to a tour company or something. You could start a side business, researching and planning private sightseeing trips for people who come here on vacation."

Sierra appreciated Amy's attempt to support her efforts, but she hadn't expected either reaction from her friends. "Maybe you guys don't understand," she said, closing her notebook and setting it aside. "This is Paul I'm talking about. I haven't seen him in a year. He's coming for only four days. I've never done anything with him. I don't know what he might like to do while he's here. His only hobby in Scotland was hiking. He might want to hike here, or he might be sick of hiking and just want to go to the movies. I need to be prepared for anything. I don't want to spend half of our four days sitting around trying to decide what to do."

Vicki's expression cleared to tender seriousness. "You're right. You're exactly right. I think you did the best thing you could have, considering the circumstances. It'll really help you both to make the most of the time." With a sparkle in her eyes, she added, "Just don't pull out the notebook the minute he walks in the door. It might scare him off."

"Don't worry," Sierra said. "This information is for my benefit. Paul doesn't even know I have the notebook." Until Vicki had said that, Sierra hadn't thought of her elaborate planning as something that would overwhelm Paul. Secretly, she was glad Vicki had mentioned her concern, or most likely Sierra would have pulled it out the first day and coaxed Paul to go through it with her to plan their time.

"I guess I need to relax a little about this, huh?" Sierra said, sipping her cup of peppermint tea. She didn't feel like eating any of their cinnamon roll today and motioned for Vicki and Amy to pull it closer to the two of them so they could split it. "You're right."

Vicki reached for a napkin and dabbed at a dot of frosting that stuck to her upper lip. "Right about what? What did we say?"

"It's what you both wanted to say but were kind enough not to say aloud. I need to back off. My mind and emotions are running away from me."

Vicki and Amy exchanged cautious glances.

"Don't shut down," Amy said. "Everything you're feeling and doing is fine. Just maybe do it and feel it all a little slower."

Sierra was surprised at the wise words from her friend. "Thanks, Amy," she said, giving Amy's wrist a squeeze. "You both have to remember I'm the inexperienced one when it comes to this whole dating thing. Do either of you have any advice for me?"

Now Amy was the one to laugh and Vicki was the one who turned serious.

"What?" Sierra asked, not sure why her innocent question caused such a reaction.

"Do we have any advice for you?" Amy said. "Look out, Sierra! You asked for it."

With heads bent close, Vicki and Amy started to advise Sierra as though they were helping her cram for the most important final of her senior year.

chapter seven

*I*T WAS **6:10** BEFORE SIERRA CAME UP FOR AIR FROM their intense powwow. She leaned back and gave a summary review to her tutors. "Okay, let me see if I've got this right. All guys are jerks, but we love them anyway. Don't ever tell them what you're really thinking because they won't understand and they'll use it against you later in an argument. Let the guy pay most of the time, and expect to be disappointed."

Vicki nodded. "That's about it."

"Oh, and if he uses the word 'love,' it's only because he wants something—so watch it," Amy said.

Sierra shook her head. "You two are pathetic."

Vicki and Amy looked shocked.

"How could you become so cynical when you're so young?"

"Reality, Sierra. You really ought to try it sometime." Amy looked serious.

"Listen, I'm sorry you both have had such terrible experiences with guys, but they're not all like that."

"How about this, Miss Innocence and Bliss?" Vicki

asked, twisting her silky brown hair up and securing it to the back of her head with a clip. "We'll meet here next Monday, and you can tell us where we're wrong."

"Not next Monday," Sierra said. "Paul will still be here."

"Okay, then the following Monday. Or maybe we'll have to call an emergency meeting after he leaves to give you the opportunity to prove us wrong."

"You'll see him at my house this Friday at the dinner party. You'll see then how wrong you are."

"Speaking of the dinner party," Amy said, "how many people are coming for sure?"

They spent the next 15 minutes discussing the guest list, menu, and preparation plans. Sierra had overlooked a few items such as drinks, bread, and when the food was going to be prepared.

Amy stepped in and gave her suggestions. Obviously, she had thought about this a lot more than Sierra had. Amy offered to bring a tray of appetizers in the morning, which Sierra could pull out after graduation. As soon as the ceremony was over, Amy would drive to the restaurant, pick up the rest of the food, and bring it to the house so it would be hot and ready to go. Vicki volunteered to collect money from everyone so Amy would have cash on Friday to pay her uncle. Sierra would take care of getting the house ready. Whatever else needed to be done, they would do together after graduation.

"At this point," Sierra said, "Warner is the only one who can't come." She forced herself not to say anything about how that didn't bother her one bit, since Warner bugged her so much. "I thought I'd ask Wesley if he wants to join us, which I know you guys wouldn't mind."

Amy seemed to light up. "That's fine with me."

Sierra wanted to say, "I knew it would be," but instead she just added, "And I don't think I told you guys, but Tawni and Jeremy might come. They're planning to drive, but Tawni still has some scheduling logistics to settle. She's supposed to do a shoot on Wednesday, which means they would have to drive straight through if they want to arrive on time Friday. If they do come, would you mind if they ate with us, too? I thought Paul might enjoy having his brother there."

"I'll need to know by tomorrow," Amy said, "so I can order enough food."

"Okay, I'll call Tawni tonight."

"I hate to be the one to break this up," Vicki said, "but I'm supposed to be home in five minutes, and this is not the week I want to get put on restriction. I've been late on my curfews twice in the last week, so I gotta fly." She stood and grabbed her backpack off the peg on the wall behind them. "I love you guys. I'll see you later." With a swish, Vicki was out the door.

"I'd better go, too," Amy said, beginning to get up.

Sierra reached for Amy's hand to stop her. "We didn't talk about God."

Amy's winsome grin inched its way across her face. "Oh, really? Maybe another time."

Sierra wasn't sure if that meant Amy was more open to talking about God or if she was feeling relieved the topic had never come up.

"I'll see you Friday morning, then," Sierra said as she

also rose from the table. "Call me if you need anything before then."

"When does Paul arrive?"

"Late Thursday night. So I don't know if I'll see him Friday morning or if he'll just show up at graduation or what."

. "It's too bad you can't call him to find out."

As Sierra drove home, she thought of how she could call Paul if she wanted. Of course, it was too early in the morning in Scotland to phone right then. She would have to wait until later that night. Where could she get the number? From Uncle Mac?

When she stepped in the door, Mrs. Jensen called from the kitchen, "Sierra, is that you?"

"Yes."

"Good. Can you come in here? I have some news."

Sierra found her mom washing dishes. A paper plate with three taquitos, rice, and beans covered with clear wrapping waited for Sierra on the counter.

"The boys had softball games, so we ate early, and Dad took them. You've had several calls. Paul called."

"He did? I was just thinking of phoning him. When did he call?"

"I'm not sure. Earlier today. He said his travel plans had changed. I wrote it all down. Do you see it on the note there?"

Sierra eagerly reached for the piece of notepaper with the little birdhouse in the top left corner. On it her mom had written the information about Paul's flight. The arrival time was listed as 4:15 P.M., and Sierra said, "This is great!

Before he wasn't getting in until after 10:00."

"Actually," Mrs. Jensen said, drying her hands and coming over to explain the note, "he doesn't arrive till Friday. I went over the schedule with him. He's sorry about missing your graduation ceremony, but he'll come right from the airport to your dinner party."

"That's okay," Sierra said. She was a little disappointed, since she had pictured him being at her graduation, but she would rather he be at the party.

"He said something about the airline changing the schedule, so he really couldn't do anything about it," Mrs. Jensen said.

"That's okay. I'm just glad he's still coming for a few days."

"Well, that's the best part. Tawni also called, and her shoot was rescheduled, so she and Jeremy are driving up from San Diego tomorrow. They'll stay with some friends of his parents in the San Francisco area and then arrive here late Wednesday night. They'll be here for the family party on Thursday, and then Paul will ride back with them next week."

"When are they going back?"

"That's what I was saying was the good part. It's open at this point. Paul might stay more than three or four days."

Sierra smiled. Her mother must have known how important this news would be. Sierra knew her mom loved going to the boys' softball games and cheering from her lawn chair, especially on warm, clear evenings like this one, but she had stayed home to give Sierra the information personally. Sierra smiled some more.

"You had another call from Margo," Mrs. Jensen said. "She won't be able to come until later Friday because her family is going out to dinner after graduation, but they said she could come here for dessert."

"I'd better tell Amy. She's ordering all the food tomorrow. Randy might not be here for dinner, either. His parents are still trying to decide."

"Would it help if I gave them a call to let them know what the plan is?" Sierra's mom asked.

"I don't know. It couldn't hurt, I guess."

"Well, do you and Amy need anything else? I thought you would probably use the good china. We're down to 21 dinner plates after that fiasco at Christmas. Do you think that will be enough?"

"That should be plenty."

"Remember that Tawni will be here in two days, in case you want to plan your expedition to find her bed before then."

"Cute, Mom. Very funny. Actually, my room isn't that bad."

Mrs. Jensen raised an eyebrow. She was a trim woman with short hair and nice lips the same shape as Sierra's. Whenever Mrs. Jensen raised an eyebrow, her lips curled up. Even though the eyebrow was supposed to communicate that she meant business, the overall look was too sweet. It always made Sierra feel like laughing.

"Okay, okay. I'll take a shovel up there tonight and see what I can unearth. Right after I eat, though."

Sierra ended up putting a little extra effort into cleaning her room over the next few days. Paul might tour the house, and that gave her a whole new motivation for straightening things up.

By the time Tawni and Jeremy arrived at 8:30 on Wednesday night, Sierra was adding the finishing touches to the bedroom. She had picked flowers from the backyard garden and was carrying the two vases upstairs when the front door opened and Tawni's clear voice called out, "We're here! Anybody home?"

Sierra hurried to put the flowers in her room—one on the nightstand next to Tawni's bed and one on a dish on top of her dresser. The calm evening breeze breathed through the open windows, and the room swirled with the flowers' refreshing fragrance.

Dashing back down the stairs, Sierra greeted her sister with a big hug. Tawni responded with a kiss on the cheek and an extra tight squeeze.

Tawni seemed taller than Sierra remembered. Was it her shoes? She was definitely slimmer. Perhaps it was the poise and posture she had developed over the months she had been working as a professional model. Her hair was cut just above her shoulders and was as close to its normal color as Sierra had seen in a while. Tawni had colored it everything from white blonde to mahogany red in the past. But today it was a soft brown, the shade of hot tea with a splash of cream stirred in. The color complemented Tawni's fair complexion.

"Are you excited?" Tawni asked.

Sierra knew her older sister most likely was referring to graduation. But when Sierra answered, "Yes, of course

I am!" she had a glimmer in her eyes because she was thinking of seeing Paul.

Paul's older brother, Jeremy, stood next to Tawni and opened his arms, inviting Sierra to give him a hug, too. She did so a little awkwardly. It felt strange to hug Paul's brother when all she had been dreaming of was hugging Paul. It was like eating imitation vanilla ice milk when she had her heart set on homemade Rocky Road ice cream. Just not the same, yet oddly similar in some ways.

Sierra tried hard to remember if Paul was taller than Jeremy was. Was Paul's hair that dark? No, she remembered it being lighter. Paul's eyes weren't as deep-set as Jeremy's, and Paul's chin was less pronounced. In Sierra's opinion, she certainly had the better-looking of the two brothers. She only let herself roll that thought over for a second because it suddenly seemed quite possible that Jeremy was standing there thinking the same thing of her—that he had gotten the better-looking of the two sisters.

Mr. and Mrs. Jensen, who had been the first to greet the weary travelers, were now asking all the usual questions about how the trip was and if they wanted something to eat.

"I'm just ready for some sleep," Tawni said. "The people we stayed with last night had a brand-new puppy, and it kept me awake all night."

"You both must be exhausted," Mrs. Jensen said.

"Not me," Jeremy said. "I slept on the living room couch last night, which was upstairs, and Tawni was in the guest room, which was right next to the garage where the puppy howled. I slept great." He put his arm around Tawni and teased her. "I kept telling Tawni to take a nap in the car, but she's not one for sleeping in moving vehicles, is she?"

Tawni shook her head, as if coaxing him not to tell the rest of the story.

But Jeremy plunged forward. "Every time I stopped at a gas station, she would fall dead asleep. Then as soon as I started the car, she would wake up. As long as she was awake, I convinced her to drive the last few hours, and I slept. So I'm wide awake, and she's about ready to drop."

"Why don't you just go up to bed?" Mr. Jensen asked. "I'll be glad to take your luggage up for you."

"I've got it," Jeremy said, using both hands to lift the heavy bag and haul it up the stairs. He hit the side of the stairwell, and Sierra saw her mom cringe. "Which room is it?" Jeremy asked.

Sierra and Tawni followed him up the stairs, and Sierra scurried ahead of him to open the bedroom door. Jeremy stood back, allowing Tawni to enter first before he let the heavy suitcase rest on the floor.

"I don't believe it," Tawni said, glancing around. "I've never seen this room look so tidy! Did you hire a maid?"

"Very funny," Sierra said.

Tawni sat on the edge of her old bed and admired the vase of blue bearded irises. "Maybe my little sister is finally growing up after all and learning to be responsible. I just never thought I'd see the day."

Something inside Sierra snapped. She and Tawni were suddenly back to their old selves, ready to fight about anything. What made it worse was that Sierra had thought they were over that stage of their lives. Now, here she was, being treated like a child in front of Jeremy.

A frightening realization came to her. It could be like this all weekend. Having Tawni there to remind Sierra that she was the lowly little sister could mean a weekend of embarrassing situations not only in front of Jeremy but also with Paul. Plus Sierra wouldn't have her private retreat all to herself for days. Tawni had invaded her room and, from all appearances, was about to invade her life.

chapter eight

SIERRA WAS GLAD TO GO TO SCHOOL ON THURSDAY morning. Many of her friends were ditching, since it was the last day and it seemed pointless to attend class. But Sierra wanted to get out of the house.

Tawni had gone to sleep early but woke up a little cranky when Sierra started opening drawers at 7:05. Sierra still hadn't gotten over the slump she had fallen into the night before. It all seemed so unreal. School was over. High school was over. A whole chunk of her childhood was over.

It came to an end so fast, Sierra thought as she drove to school. *I can remember my first day of school when Mom made me wear those little red shoes with the buckles. I hated those shoes! What was she thinking when she bought those for me? Or did she buy them? They were probably hand-me-downs.*

Pulling into the school parking lot, Sierra realized that, to her mother's credit, she might not have understood Sierra's preferences then, but she sure understood them now. Sierra thought her mom was great to be willing to adjust the family's graduation celebration so Sierra could

spend Friday night with her friends. Vicki's parents had
made a big issue of the arrangement, and Vicki said they
had had a huge argument over it.

Sierra felt extra appreciative of her mom, yet at the
same time a little melancholy. On her first day of school
many years ago, pancakes had been served for breakfast, a
love note had been tucked into her sweater pocket, and
photographs had been taken before she walked down the
sidewalk in a straight line behind Tawni, who was behind
Wesley, who was behind Cody. Today she had made her
own breakfast—a banana. No one had even said good-bye
to her, and she had driven to school alone. Not that she
expected her mom to take pictures. It was all just so different from the rest of her school experience.

If this was what being grown-up and independent was
all about, Sierra wasn't sure she liked it. Or at least she
wasn't sure she wanted to be at this point yet in her life.

Her last day of school was one party after another in
each of her classes. Most of her teachers had nice speeches
they gave to the students about what a wonderful year it
had been. One of her teachers handed out cards with a
Bible verse as a blessing for their future. It was a fun, sweet,
sad, strange sort of day.

Instead of driving directly home, Sierra stopped at
Eaton's Pharmacy. A little soda fountain with red vinyl
stools was located inside the corner drugstore. She ordered
a chocolate shake. It was served along with a silver shake
canister containing the portion of the drink that wouldn't
fit in the glass. The server was the same waitress who had
been there the first time Sierra had visited the fountain

with Granna Mae. Sierra didn't remember the woman's name but smiled and answered questions about how her family was doing, especially Granna Mae.

Sierra slurped slowly in the quiet shop and remembered when Granna Mae had brought her here a year and a half ago, after her first day at Royal Academy. Granna Mae traditionally took her children to Eaton's for a shake on their first day of school. It didn't matter that Sierra started Royal in the middle of the year; she still qualified for a chocolate shake with Granna Mae at Eaton's.

Now Sierra felt strange sitting here alone and grown-up and responsible and not doted on by anyone. She knew she wouldn't feel this way once the family party started that night. Tomorrow would be graduation and Paul's arrival and the start of their days together. That's when she would love being grown-up and responsible and having the freedom to do what she wanted.

But for this singular moment, she was a sad, lonely graduating senior—so sad and lonely she couldn't finish her shake.

She left an exorbitant tip on the counter, feeling that someone needed to reward that woman for working in the same drugstore during Sierra's entire high school career.

Then Sierra drove home, convincing herself that the best years of her life were still to come. She wondered if part of the sadness came from her not growing up in Portland but being a transplant in the middle of her junior year. She loved her friends dearly, but she didn't feel the same about them as she did about the friends she had grown up with in the little town of Pineville in northern

California. She had thought she would stay in touch with them. When Sierra moved, she had made earnest promises about going back for her friends' graduation. She knew every one of the 59 students who had graduated there last weekend, and she had known most of them her whole life. But Sierra was surprised by how quickly she had moved on and forgotten all her promises about visiting. Most of her friends had moved on quickly, too. Only two or three had sent her graduation announcements, and none of them had included a note.

As far as Sierra knew, neither she nor her mom had sent her graduation announcement to any of her old friends in Pineville. It made her sad.

How can things change like that? It won't be like that when I go to college, will it? Even though Amy doesn't have any interest in going to Rancho Corona, and even if Vicki ends up not being accepted, we'll still be good friends, won't we? When I come home for vacation, the three of us will still get together at Mama Bear's. We just have to! I refuse to believe our friendship could dissolve.

By the time Sierra walked into the house, she was in a "blue funk," as Amy once described an especially depressed mood. If some category at the Academy Awards existed for graduating seniors who act happy at the family party while they are in a level-two blue funk, Sierra would have won that year. She put on the best show she could for her loving family. Her older brothers, Cody and Wes, were both there. Cody's wife, Katrina, and their son, Tyler, showered Sierra with hugs as if she had won some talent show instead of merely graduating from high school. The hugs felt funny from Katrina because she was six and a half months pregnant. Sierra wasn't used to hugging pregnant women.

Twice during the evening Katrina took Sierra's hand, pressed it to her abdomen, and said, "There. Did you feel that? Wait. She'll kick again."

Sierra didn't know how to tell her well-meaning sister-in-law that she would love her new niece to pieces once she made a grand appearance that summer. For now, though, Sierra wasn't big on bonding through tracking the baby's tiny kicks across Katrina's bubbled-out belly.

Mrs. Jensen made a huge dinner with salads and vegetable trays, and Mr. Jensen grilled chicken. A big carrot cake with cream cheese frosting was served. It had plastic decorations of a graduation cap and rolled-up diploma on top, along with the words, "Congratulations, Sierra!"

Everyone gave Sierra gifts. Cards and money were presented from relatives who hadn't come. Granna Mae was wonderfully bright and coherent throughout the evening. And Sierra noted that Jeremy fit right in with the festivities and treated Tawni like a princess.

A letter had arrived that day announcing that Sierra had been awarded another scholarship, her fourth. Everything was ideal, and she should have been as happy as she pretended to be.

Instead, she felt numb. All the celebrating seemed to be for someone else, one of the older Jensen children, like all the graduation parties had been in years past. She was just one of the many kids at the party. Only she wasn't one of the "little" ones anymore. Sierra sensed she had crossed some invisible line and was now one of the "older" Jensen kids. Gavin and Dillon were the only little ones left of the six kids, and they had a long way to go before they graduated from high school.

Not until the next morning did Sierra believe it was all really happening. Her mom had hung Sierra's cap and gown on the back of her closet door; when Sierra woke up, they were the first things she saw. She remembered when she had tried on Tawni's cap two years ago and thought it was the silliest-looking hat in the world. She had swung her head to make the tassel do a hula. Tawni had yelled at her, and that was that.

This morning the hat hanging on the back of the closet door was hers, and she thought it looked rather important and dignified. She knew she probably would yell at Gavin if he tried to make her tassel dance a silly hula on his unscholarly head.

This was the day she had long awaited. Paul was on an airplane this very minute, and before the day was over, she would see him and . . .

She forced her imagination to shut down. All in good time, she coached herself, using one of Granna Mae's familiar lines.

Sierra prayed as she showered, dressed, and tried to get her hair to cooperate. After spending an extra minute with the mascara wand, she went downstairs, where she found Jeremy and Wes engaged in serious battle with a video game.

"You guys are pathetic," she teased. Neither of them

had showered yet, and both had wacky hair and wore crumpled T-shirts and shorts.

"Hey, don't make fun of our male-bonding rituals," Jeremy said.

"Yeah," Wes agreed. "Do we break into your little tea parties and tell you you're pathetic?"

"No. My apologies. Bond away, big boys."

"Whoa!" Wes said, bobbing and ducking with the controller in his hand. "You shouldn't have gotten that one, Jeremy. I was in there way ahead of you. Whoa, look out!"

Jeremy laughed. "You snooza, you looza."

Sierra smiled on her way into the kitchen. Paul would fit in nicely with this clan, especially since his own big brother was already part of the gang. Mom had set out a basket of muffins, a pitcher of fresh orange juice, and a big bowl of fruit salad. Bright, golden sunshine tumbled through the open kitchen window, lighting up the counter. Sierra could hear four-year-old Tyler in the backyard with his grandpa, laughing his adorable laugh. Brutus was barking and probably slobbering all over Tyler. Someone upstairs was running a shower. A blow dryer ran at top speed in the downstairs bathroom.

Even though Sierra was the only one in the kitchen as she poured her orange juice, she felt surrounded by love. At times like this she enjoyed being in a big family and thought that anyone who didn't come from such a clan was really missing out.

The extended family had to take three cars to fit everyone in for the ride to Sierra's school auditorium. Sierra rode with Tawni and Jeremy. Fortunately, Tawni had slept in, so she was in the best of moods. If Sierra needed to tell Tawni that she and Paul wanted to do something alone rather than with Tawni and Jeremy, it seemed more likely her sister would understand now that she was in a cheery mood.

Sierra had laid her gown across her legs with her cap balanced on her lap. She felt nervous, but she wasn't sure why. She didn't think it was graduation. After all, she wasn't valedictorian, so she didn't have to make a speech or anything. All she had to do was walk up to the podium, shake the principal's hand, take her diploma, and walk down the stage. So why did she feel queasy?

It has to be Paul, she thought. *I'm so nervous and excited about seeing him I can hardly think about anything else. But graduation is something a person should probably pay attention to!*

She tried to imagine what Paul was doing on the plane right now. Was he sleeping? Reading? Or gazing out the plane's window, just as she was gazing out the car's window? Was he feeling nervous about seeing her?

When the car pulled into the school parking lot, Sierra put aside all her thoughts of Paul, separated from her family, and scurried with her cap and gown to the school library, where all the girls were meeting before the ceremony.

Vicki was already there, wearing her gown and adjusting her cap. She gave a happy squeal and dashed over to hug Sierra when she walked in. Several other girls greeted Sierra with hugs and nervous laughter. They helped each other get their caps on right, and Margo said, "Whoever thought up this flat-head style anyhow? I don't know why someone didn't come up with something better. I mean, really, they can put men on the moon, but they can't design a decent hat for the masses to wear when they receive a diploma."

Sierra decided this would be a good time to demonstrate her talent of making her tassel do the hula. Vicki was the first one to notice and tried to imitate the subtle head motions that set the tassel swaying just right. Two more girls copied them, and then three more came over and joined the impromptu competition. Ripples of laughter rolled over the group, providing a release for their nervous energy.

"Which side is this tassel supposed to be on?" one girl asked.

"This side," Vicki said, demonstrating. "Don't you remember them telling us at practice? Then we flip it at the very end of the ceremony."

One of the history teachers entered the library and clapped her hands. "All right, ladies, this is it. Line up alphabetically in the hall. Shall we go now? Nice and orderly."

The guys were already lined up in the hall, with big gaps where they remembered girls being from the practice session. The boys looked as if they had been goofing around, too. At practice, strict warnings had been given to all the students about attempting pranks during the ceremony. The year before some girls had smuggled bottles of soap bubbles into the auditorium and had filled the air with bubbles. The harmless trick caused more trouble than it was worth, so this year the administration had come down hard about no shenanigans of any kind. Sierra wondered if the rule would be respected.

"Sierra, over here," Randy called to her. At practice, they had discovered for the first time that they were next to each other alphabetically at Royal Academy. Sierra slipped in line between her buddy and a guy she didn't know very well who was fiddling with the tie he had on underneath his gown.

"You nervous?" Randy asked. His half grin was broader than usual.

"No," Sierra said. "Are you?"

"Naw, I've been looking forward to this."

"Me, too," she agreed.

"All right, everyone, listen up." The football coach's booming voice echoed down the hall. "Let's go. Exactly as you did it in practice. This is it. Go make your mamas proud."

The auditorium's doors opened, and the music rushed out to welcome them inside. The line of students, all wearing deep blue caps and gowns, began to march down the hallway.

Just as they were to move forward, Randy reached back and took Sierra's hand. As the music played, Sierra walked down the aisle, holding hands with her best buddy, Randy.

chapter nine

FTER THREE SONGS AND A SPEECH FROM A MAN who had graduated from Royal Academy and now ran a chain of furniture stores in Arizona, the principal finally moved to the podium. Sierra blew air out past her protruding lower lip in an effort to cool off her perspiring forehead. The auditorium was stuffy, and the cap and gown made her feel a little claustrophobic. Fortunately, the awards and special recognitions went quickly. The last award was a new one they had added this year for the student who had best demonstrated Christian character during his or her stay at Royal.

"It'll probably go to you," Randy whispered.

"Hardly," Sierra whispered back. "You're the one who stopped the school riot last fall when you voluntarily cut your hair."

Before they could argue any more, the principal announced, "And the winner of this award will receive a $4,000 scholarship, which was generously donated by Pell-mer's Furniture of Arizona, to the college of his or her choice. The recipient is . . . Randy Jenkins."

Randy nearly rocketed out of his chair. He gave Sierra a huge grin and playful tag on the shoulder before going up to the podium to receive the envelope and to shake hands.

This is so perfect, God! Sierra thought exultantly. *You knew how much Randy needed scholarship money for Rancho. You are so awesome! Thank You, thank You!*

Randy returned to his seat, looking as if the reality of the award had just sunk in. He was more dazed than when he first had heard the announcement.

"That was a total God-thing," Sierra whispered.

"Yeah," was all Randy could say.

The calling of the graduates' names began, and row by row the students went forward. By the time Sierra stepped onto the podium, she didn't feel nervous at all. Out of the corner of her eye, she noticed the camera's flash as her mom captured the moment on film. Sierra smiled, accepted the diploma in her left hand, and remembered to cross over her right hand to shake hands with the principal. That's when her English teacher, who stood at the microphone, announced Sierra's name and her scholastic rank with resounding clarity. "Sierra Mae Jensen, *magna cum laude.*"

A burst of applause followed, sending a little shiver up Sierra's spine. She paused right before going down the stairs and looked in the direction of the wildest clapping. Sure enough, there was her family and her mom with the camera. Sierra held up her diploma, smiled back, and gave her mother the chance to take a shot.

Her one moment in the spotlight ended when the name

of the next student was called, and a burst of applause for him followed. Sierra returned to her seat next to Randy. They gave each other clandestine pokes in the arm to show how proud they were of one another.

The ceremony ended without any shenanigans. After a prayer and a charge to the students, they were instructed to switch their tassels. They marched out much more triumphantly than they had entered. Sierra looked for her family as she passed their aisle and gave a special little wave to Tyler and then blew him a kiss.

As soon as they were in the hallway, a string of poppers and flying streamers were released. It was impossible to tell where the party favors had come from, but it didn't matter. Everyone was cheering and hugging and tossing the streamers back into the air. Caps and tassels were flying in the crowded hallway. A can of Silly String appeared, and suddenly Sierra had long, bright pink bits of Silly String in her hair. She was laughing so hard, she could hardly breathe. She watched Randy switch hats, putting on his black baseball cap with the long ponytail attached to the back. He placed his graduation cap on top of the baseball cap. Some other friends of theirs—Tyler, Jen, and Tara— came over, and Tara put a clip-on hoop earring in Randy's nose.

By the time the parents and other guests tried to exit into the hallway, it was impossible to calm the wild seniors. None of the teachers tried to stop the antics. Sierra wanted to think it was because the students had followed the rules through the whole ceremony. They deserved to go a little crazy at the end.

The only one who tried to yell above the crowd was the football coach. He kept directing them to take their party into the parking lot, which they eventually did.

Mrs. Jensen snapped lots of pictures of Sierra and her friends. Since Sierra didn't want to stop having fun with her friends to become the photographer, she was glad. She knew these were the snapshots she would keep in her photo album for the rest of her life.

Randy was the wackiest she had ever seen him. He climbed onto the top of the planter in front of the school and acted as if he were leading a cheer with his ponytail flapping in the wind.

Amy made her way through the crowd and greeted Vicki and Sierra with a big hug. "This is way wilder than my graduation was!" Amy yelled over the noise.

Sierra nodded and yelled back, "Where's my air horn when I need it?"

Amy laughed, sharing a not-so-fun memory with Sierra that involved an air horn and Sierra's overzealous good intentions.

Vicki put her thumb and first finger in her mouth and let out the shrillest whistle Sierra had ever heard. She covered her ears and turned to her usually polite friend. "Where did you learn to do that?"

"My dad. Here, like this. Try it!"

Amy, Sierra, and Vicki worked at improving their shrill whistling as Randy wound down his final cheer. Many of the parents were trying to coax the students to calm down and get their things together so they could leave and have a nice, respectable family dinner. Sierra's family kindly stood to the side and let her have her graduation moment with her buddies.

Vicki's dad motioned for Vicki to come along. She stopped her whistling, and after another hug for Sierra, she said, "I'll be over to your house as soon as I can, but don't try to hold any food for me."

Sierra nodded. It suddenly struck her that Paul could be here already. He could be at the airport or even on his way to her house. She didn't have her watch on, but she knew it was getting late. "I'm going to get things ready at the house," Sierra told Amy.

"I'll pick up the food now," Amy said. "What are you going to wear? Do you think this is too fancy? Should I stop at home to change?"

Sierra glanced at Amy's short, sleeveless black dress. It was fancy, but it looked great on her. "I don't know what I'm going to wear. Just wear that, and if you want to change, you can borrow something of mine."

Amy nodded and took off for her car. Sierra joined her family and gestured to Randy that she was leaving. She didn't know if he saw her, since her departure didn't stop his antics. Sierra shook her head. Ever since Randy had found out he was going to Rancho, he seemed to have gone through a personality transformation. It made her wonder if he was going to be one of those guys who go berserk once they move away to college and experience freedom from parental authority. She had never thought of his parents as overly strict, but maybe they were more so than she realized.

Sierra linked her arm with Granna Mae's and walked

to the Jensen family van. She noticed how many of the cars in the parking lot were decorated. Most of her friends had written congratulatory notes with white shoe polish on the windows of their cars or their friends' cars. Sierra had been so absorbed in the rush of the last few weeks that she hadn't even thought of decorating her little car.

"Such a to-do," Granna Mae said. "My, my, my!"

"It's so much fun!" Sierra said. "Just think, Granna Mae, I'm a graduate!"

Granna Mae gave Sierra a foggy look as if she weren't sure who Sierra was or what she was talking about. The blank look caused Sierra to hold her grandmother's arm a little tighter and make sure she got situated in the front seat of the van. Sierra whispered to her mom, "I think this was a little much for Granna Mae."

Mrs. Jensen nodded, and they all climbed into the van.

At home, Sierra didn't see any unfamiliar cars parked in front of their house, so apparently Paul hadn't arrived yet. She wanted to hurry inside to change, but her mom was set on taking a whole roll of family photos. It took only 10 minutes or so, but each minute seemed like an hour as Sierra watched every car that came down the street. None of them stopped in front of her house.

Cody, Katrina, and Tyler left after hugging everyone, and Sierra hurried up to her room. The time was exactly 4:30. Paul was in Portland. Was he still at the baggage claim? She stopped and smiled at her reflection in the mirror. When she and Paul met a year and a half ago, they had both grabbed for the same bag on the luggage carousel.

She could hardly stand the anticipation. She pictured

Uncle Mac picking Paul up and bringing him over to her house.

Sierra had no idea what to wear. She heard the doorbell ring and knew she had better hurry and decide. The dress she had worn under her robe was kind of dressy, and it was similar to Amy's. That wasn't unusual. Sierra and Amy shared the same taste in clothes. But would it seem odd for the two of them to wear the same sort of dress at a small dinner party? Sierra couldn't remember what Vicki was wearing.

The doorbell rang again, and Sierra decided she wouldn't worry about changing. She had a party to hostess and a very special guest to greet. A quick freshening-up in the bathroom was all she allowed herself before lightheartedly skipping down the stairs to see her family and friends.

A rattle of excited chatter rose from the front porch. Sierra looked through the open door and saw the back of Randy's head with the ponytail. Tawni was in the circle, as well as Jeremy, Sierra's mom, and her two little brothers. Amy stood by the steps. The group seemed focused on something on the porch.

"What is it?" Sierra asked, opening the screen door and approaching the huddle.

Tawni and Jeremy both stepped back so Sierra could see. It was the last thing she expected.

chapter ten

"They're alive," Sierra said, looking at Amy for an explanation.

"I know."

Sierra gazed at the large bucket of fidgeting red lobsters trying to climb up the slick plastic sides. "You didn't say we were going to fix live lobsters."

"I didn't know. My uncle just said 'lobster' and that he would give them to us at cost, by the pound. I thought he was going to cook them for us."

"How do you cook them?" Sierra asked.

"It's easy. You just boil them," Wesley said, coming up the steps with a second bucket. "Haven't you ever seen how they do it in the huge vats down on the coast?"

"At least you know they're fresh," Jeremy said. Tawni playfully punched him in the arm.

"How many did you get?" Sierra asked.

"Sixteen."

"Can we have two of them?" Dillon asked. "Then Gavin and I could have a race."

"Cool," Randy said. "I'm in."

"You guys!" Sierra said. "No, you may not play with our food!"

"I don't know if I can go through with this," Amy said. "I mean, I don't know if I can eat them. They were looking at me in the car on the way over."

Wes laughed. He had worked at DiGrassi's restaurant last summer as a waiter and was heartless when it came to the fresh catch of the day. "You've eaten them before at the restaurant. I've seen you."

"I know, but I never actually met any of them before I ate them."

Now everyone was laughing.

"What's this one's name?" Randy teased, picking up one of the plump fellows and holding it up for Amy to see. The claws were taped closed, but Amy pulled back as if it could pinch her.

"This one is Rory," Gavin said, bravely picking up another lobster.

"Where did you get that name?" Tawni asked.

"I dunno."

Just then a car pulled into the driveway, and Sierra moved away from the group with her heart pounding. She thought how unlike any of her dreams it would be to see Paul at this moment. She had conjured up a variety of scenarios, but none of them involved greeting Paul with half a dozen people gathered around two buckets of live lobsters.

But it wasn't Paul. It was Tre and Margo. Drake pulled in behind them. Cassie was with him, as well as Jen and Tara. Drake waved to Sierra. She waved back.

"I'm just dropping these guys off," he said. "Cassie and I are going to a party at her house, but we might come back here later."

"Okay," Sierra called back from the edge of the porch. "Have fun, and I hope you guys do come back. Hi, Cassie."

The girl in the front seat waved back at Sierra. By then the others were up the porch steps and were being introduced to their dinner.

"Can we mark them so we get the one we want? That one looks good," Tara said.

"I'm going to see if we have an extra large cooking pot in the basement," Mrs. Jensen said. "Wes, why don't you move those lobsters into the kitchen. It's hot out here on the porch. And I think they should have more water in the buckets."

Another car pulled up, and again Sierra looked expectantly at the driver. It was Warner.

I thought he said he couldn't come, she thought sullenly. She followed her mom into the house before any of her feelings about Warner showed themselves. "Did anyone listen to the answering machine since we came back?" she asked. "I was just wondering if Paul's plane was delayed or anything."

"I don't think anyone has listened yet. Your father was trying to put up the volleyball net in the backyard in case you wanted to play later."

"In dresses?" Sierra was beginning to feel as though this party were going downhill faster than a lobster could scamper out of a bucket.

"Well, later," Mrs. Jensen said, heading for the

basement. "If you end up changing. It's up to you." She took off down the stairs.

Wes entered the kitchen with the first bucket of dinner. The frightened fellows were clambering up the sides of the bucket. To Sierra, it resembled the muted sound of finger-nails on a chalkboard, and suddenly she lost her appetite.

"I still have bread in the car," Amy said as she entered the kitchen with a box of Caesar salad already prepared and packed in plastic bags. "Can you get it, Sierra?"

"I was going to check . . ." Sierra saw desperation on Amy's face and decided checking the answering machine could wait. Besides, Sierra might go to Amy's car and find Paul pulling into the driveway. "Sure," Sierra said. "Any-thing else?"

"Well, I don't want to be mean or anything, but are your brothers going to be around the whole time?" Amy looked at Sierra and seemed to notice for the first time they had on similar dresses. Amy's expression grew to a deeper level of frustration.

"Oh," Sierra teased, "you want me to tell Wesley to get lost?"

"No!" Amy said quickly. Then she looked agitated. "I meant Gavin and Dillon, and you know it."

Sierra's mom came up from the basement just then with a huge silver cooking pot. "Don't worry, Amy," Mrs. Jensen said. "This is your party. I have plans for the boys just as soon as I know you have everything you need."

Amy looked a little embarrassed. "I'm sure we have everything. Thanks."

Wes entered with the second batch of lobsters as Sierra

headed for the car to bring in the bread. She wished she knew how long it would take Paul to get through the airport. When she had come back from England, her plane had landed in San Francisco first, and that's where she had gone through customs. For some reason she remembered Jeremy saying that Paul's flight was from Heathrow to Seattle, and then he would take a hopper down to Portland. He might have missed the connection at Seattle if his international flight was delayed.

Sierra tried not to worry. They still had a lot to do before they could serve their dinner, so maybe it was a good thing Paul wasn't there yet. She carried the four bags of dinner rolls in her arms and joined the rest of the group in the kitchen.

Everyone was at work. Tawni wore an apron and was trying to talk Jeremy into wearing one, too, but he wasn't cooperating. Randy was filling the cooking pot with water. Wes was cleaning up a mess he had made on the floor while trying to add more water to the lobster buckets. Warner was taking Amy's orders on where to place the croutons on the salad plates, which Margo was preparing by pulling salad from the bags with tongs. Tre was unwrapping a cube of butter and putting it on a plate Amy had set out earlier when she had brought over the appetizers.

For a moment, Sierra stood and watched this organized circus. How did Amy do it? Sierra never could have gotten so many people to work together so easily.

"Bread, Aim. Where do you want it?"

"Does your mom have two or three bread baskets we could use?"

Sierra went searching for the baskets. Sierra's mom and younger brothers had disappeared, and Sierra thought it best not to involve her mom, especially when Sierra certainly could find some baskets on her own.

Tawni was the one who finally remembered where they were. Mrs. Jensen had changed some things around in the kitchen after the oven had caught on fire last Thanksgiving. With the bread in baskets lined with Granna Mae's white linen napkins, Sierra joined Tawni in the dining room to set the table with the old family china.

"What's the final count?" Tawni asked.

"I'm not sure."

Just then the doorbell rang, and Sierra's heart stopped. She and Tawni exchanged knowing looks of anticipation, and Tawni nodded for Sierra to answer the door.

"Someone's at the door," Warner called out from the kitchen. "Want me to get it?"

"Let Sierra," Tawni yelled back.

With light steps, Sierra hurried to the door. Her heart pounded all the way up to her inner ears. She put her hand on the doorknob, paused a moment, moistened her suddenly dry lips, and cleared her throat. Pulling open the door and putting on her best smile, Sierra sang out, "Hi!"

A gangly young boy stood on the doormat with a receipt pad in his hand. His bike lay on its side in the front yard. Apparently, Sierra's disappointment showed instantly because the boy's smile turned to a half grin of conciliation.

"Collecting for the *Oregonian?*" He said it with a question mark at the end, as if he somehow knew he should apologize.

"Could you please come back tomorrow?" Sierra tried to find a smile for him and to sound pleasant. "No one is here right now who can pay you."

The boy nodded and scampered away. He mounted his bike like a fleeing outlaw and took off into the sunset. Sierra quickly scanned the street for cars. There were none. She closed the door and turned around.

All her friends burst out laughing. They had formed a haphazard pyramid in an effort to watch her reunion with Paul.

"The paper boy!" Amy exclaimed, giggling.

"Did you see the look on that poor kid's face?" Randy said with a hoot. "He couldn't get out of here fast enough."

"Very funny," Sierra said, finding it impossible to hold back her smile. She spotted the camera on the entry table and said, "Wait, you guys. Don't move." Quickly focusing, she snapped a shot of her friends, who were all crammed into the entrance to the living room, looking like one strange, aproned body with eight heads. "Let me get another one," she said before they all lost their balance. "Hold it! Smile!"

Sierra was about to take the picture when she caught sight of something out of the corner of her eye moving toward her from the kitchen. She held the camera in place and glanced at the moving object on the floor. An escapee from the dinner bucket was flailing its way toward the front door. Sierra wanted to scream but decided she would play a joke back on her friends.

"Okay, just hold it. I'm trying to focus," Sierra said, stalling for time.

"Hurry up, I'm going to fall over!"

"My leg is asleep!"

"Sierra, I have an elbow in my ear!"

"Take the picture!"

With one eye on the lobster, Sierra slowly counted under her breath, "Three, two, one!" Right on cue, the runaway lobster scurried past the human pyramid. They all noticed it at the same time and reacted wildly. That's when Sierra snapped the picture.

She burst out laughing as Wesley lunged for the crawling crustacean and the whole pyramid crumbled. Sierra took another picture. The phone rang, and she broke away from the human pileup to answer it, but her father already had. He was in the kitchen, which made her wonder if the escapee had had a little help.

"Yes," her dad said, "this is Howard Jensen."

Sierra looked around the kitchen to see what else needed to be done to prepare dinner—besides cooking the lobsters.

"Oh, yes. How are you? Oh?"

Not seeing anything else needing to be done, Sierra went back to the entryway to put away the camera and check if the meals on wheels had been captured. The whole group was laughing hysterically as Wes pretended to wrestle with the lobster.

"I'm not eating that one," Sierra said.

"Let's mark it and make sure Wes has to eat it," Tawni suggested. She had stepped away from the group. Roughhousing was not her idea of a good time.

"Tawni, Sierra," Mr. Jensen called from the kitchen,

"could you come here a moment, please?"

Tawni and Sierra exchanged glances. They both had noticed the slight catch in his voice. Tawni followed Sierra to the kitchen. Mr. Jensen had hung up the phone. He had a strange look on his face.

"What is it?" Sierra asked. "Is it Paul?"

"Tawni," Mr. Jensen said quietly, "could you ask Jeremy to come here? I'd like to talk to the three of you."

Before Tawni could turn around, Jeremy stepped into the kitchen. The rest of the group was still laughing in the entryway. The kitchen was silent except for the boiling water in the pot on the stove.

"That was your uncle Mac," Mr. Jensen said, looking at Jeremy.

Sierra felt as if icy fingers had reached down her throat and were trying to yank out her heart. Her father wouldn't look like this or sound like this unless something was wrong—seriously wrong. Sierra felt her world screeching to a halt as she waited for her father to speak.

He closed his eyes as he said, "There's been a plane crash."

chapter eleven

"How? Where? When? What do you know?" Sierra's mind raced. She shot out questions while the others remained silent.

Mr. Jensen opened his eyes. Tears glistened in them. That's when Sierra began to panic.

"Paul's plane out of Heathrow crash-landed in Seattle," her father said. "It happened at 3:00 this afternoon. Apparently, the plane made it to the runway but caught on fire. So far they haven't found any survivors."

Sierra felt her body slump slowly to the floor. Tawni and Jeremy wrapped their arms around each other and leaned against the wall.

"My parents?" Jeremy said.

"Mac is trying to reach them."

"I'm going to Seattle," Jeremy suddenly said. He reached for the phone. "I'll see if Uncle Mac wants to go with me." He punched in the numbers, and Sierra buried her face in her hands. She had no tears. Only pain. The sharpest, most unbelievable pain she had ever felt in her life, right in the middle of her chest.

The uninformed guests paraded into the kitchen, and Mr. Jensen spoke to Wesley in hushed tones. The others heard as well. Instantly, the group fell silent. Randy came over and sat on the floor next to Sierra. He didn't say anything.

Jeremy hung up the phone and said, "My uncle is going with me. We'll drive up to Seattle."

"Do you want me to go?" Tawni asked.

"Yes."

Sierra looked up.

"Unless you think you should stay here with Sierra," Jeremy added.

Tawni and Sierra exchanged glances for the third time that evening. This time both of them had red eyes.

"Go," Sierra said hoarsely. She wanted them to include her, to know that she would want to go, too. But she knew that was asking too much. She was supposed to be hosting a party at the moment. And besides, what was she to Paul?

"Hey, it's on TV," Warner said. He had left the kitchen and turned the TV in the living room to the local news channel, expecting them all to congratulate his quick thinking.

Mr. Jensen and Wes slowly moved into the living room with the others. Jeremy hesitated; then he bolted into the room with Tawni right behind him. Only Sierra and Randy remained in the kitchen. Neither of them spoke. Randy reached over and took Sierra's hand in his and held it. It struck Sierra that he had reached for her hand a few hours ago when they were entering the auditorium, ready to graduate. Her whole world had been different then.

The news was turned up loud, and they could hear the reporter. "Flight 8079 out of Heathrow experienced failure with the landing gear when it arrived at SeaTac at 3:07 this afternoon. As you can see from this earlier clip, the rescue crew began evacuation immediately. However, due to the explosion that occurred when the plane's nose hit the runway, extensive damage was done in a short time. We have been informed that so far 157 fatalities and three survivors are confirmed. We will keep you updated as the information comes to us. Back to you, Bob."

Sierra squeezed Randy's hand. "Three survivors!" She jumped up and ran into the living room.

"Three survivors!" Jeremy repeated when he saw Sierra.

"I heard." Inwardly, Sierra began to pray with all her might, *Oh, please, God! Let Paul be one of the three. Let him be okay. Don't let him die!*

"Did they say which hospital the survivors are in?" Mr. Jensen asked.

Wes had already gone for the cordless phone. "I'll find out," he said.

Mr. Jensen took the remote control from Warner and began to check other channels. There was a report on another channel with a rerun of the crashed plane, nose to the pavement, still in flames, with rescue workers rushing into it. Sierra had only heard the description from the kitchen floor. Now, seeing the pictures, she realized it was even more horrible than she had imagined. Black smoke billowed from the sides of the plane as sirens wailed.

The doorbell rang, and Sierra rushed with Tawni and

Jeremy to greet Uncle Mac. Sierra impulsively ran into his
arms and hugged him tightly, as if he were the recipient of
the hug she had intended for Paul.

"They said there are three survivors," Jeremy said.

"Really?" Uncle Mac came into the living room with
the rest of them.

"Wesley's trying to reach the hospital," Mr. Jensen said,
shaking hands with Uncle Mac.

"Did you contact my parents?" Jeremy asked.

"No, I kept getting the answering machine, and I didn't
want to leave a message."

"They're at Emmanuel Hospital," Wes said, hanging up.
"They won't release any information over the phone, but
if you go there and you're related, they will let you in."

Tawni and Jeremy exchanged tentative looks. Sierra
knew they must be thinking, *And what if Paul isn't one of
them?*

"I'm ready to go," Uncle Mac said. "Who else is going?"

"Tawni and me," Jeremy said. "We'd better grab an
overnight bag."

"That's right," Tawni said. "Sierra, can you help me
pack some things?"

The two sisters made their way up the stairs in single
file. "Mom doesn't know," Sierra said, suddenly feeling
dizzy. "Where is she?"

"She took the boys miniature golfing. Do you have a
small bag I could borrow?"

"Sure." Sierra retrieved the bag, and neither of them
spoke as Tawni transferred several neatly folded T-shirts

and a pair of jeans into the bag, along with enough under-
wear for three days.

"You'll call as soon as you get there, won't you?"

"Yes," Tawni promised.

"I mean, even if it's the worst, you have to call me
immediately and tell me."

"I will."

With no warning, the tears came coursing down Sierra's
cheeks. She had so much she wanted to say as Tawni took
her in her arms and held her close. "He wanted to go into
ministry, Tawni. He got his life right with God." A huge
sob overwhelmed Sierra. "He was coming to Portland
to . . ." She couldn't speak. Breaking away from Tawni,
Sierra went for Paul's treasured letter, which she had kept
under her pillow since the day it had arrived. She held it
out for Tawni to read.

Tawni read the first page and then slowly sank to her
bed's edge. "Oh, Sierra," she murmured.

Tawni was on the last page, reading the poem, when a
soft knock sounded on their door. Jeremy cautiously
opened the door. "Uncle Mac is ready."

Tawni was awash in tears and motioned for Jeremy to
come in. Now Tawni was the one who couldn't speak. She
held out the letter to Jeremy.

"What's this?"

Sierra swallowed hard and forced her voice to cooperate. "It's a letter from Paul. It's okay for you to read it,
if you want."

Jeremy began to read aloud and then trimmed his
choking voice down to a whisper when he read the line,

"I have finally entered through that gate, and I'm finding pasture, as the verse says."

He put down the letter and wiped his eyes with the back of his hand.

"Keep reading," Tawni whispered.

Jeremy finished the letter. His tear-filled eyes went to Sierra's red face. She and Jeremy looked at each other a long minute. Then, in two quick strides, Jeremy crossed the room and took Sierra in his arms. Together they cried.

"You'll never know," Jeremy finally choked out, "what your prayers did for my brother." He held her tightly and said, "Don't stop now. Not as long as we have a shred of hope. Don't stop praying."

"I won't," Sierra promised.

They pulled apart, and Tawni stood beside them, composed but still more shaken than Sierra had ever seen her.

"And I'll be praying for you guys, too, that you have a safe trip up there," Sierra offered.

Tawni tenderly kissed Sierra on the cheek and said words Sierra had never expected. "I love you, Sierra. I love you with all my heart."

"I love you, too," Sierra said, suddenly clinging to her.

"I know," Tawni whispered, stroking Sierra's hair.

Another knock came. Mr. Jensen entered, and clearing his throat, said, "Mac's ready to go."

"We're coming," Tawni said, quickly zipping up the bag. Jeremy reached for it and suggested Tawni bring a pillow and blanket, just in case she could sleep in the car this time.

Sierra followed them to Uncle Mac's car and made

them promise to call as soon as they reached Seattle. It was a three-hour drive. She knew they would be three of the longest hours of her life, waiting for the phone to ring.

Sierra's dad wrapped his arm around her as they walked back to the house. She wanted to be alone, but there were all her dinner guests. She knew she could ask them to leave and they would understand, but Sierra didn't want them to go. She needed her friends now more than ever.

Amy was waiting for them at the front door. She tenderly reached for Sierra's hand and gave it a squeeze. "You okay?"

"I don't know," Sierra said.

"Why don't you sit down. Do you want to be alone for a while?"

Sierra was surprised at how well Amy knew her. It dawned on her that Vicki hadn't arrived yet, but when she did, just like when Sierra's mom came home, they would have to relay the awful announcement all over again.

"No, I don't want you to leave," Sierra said.

"Do you want something to eat?"

"I don't know."

Wes met them in the entryway and stood close to his little sister. "They may have found another survivor. The news just announced it. Do you want to come watch the report?"

"I don't know." Sierra stood in the middle of the hallway, suddenly exhausted and directionless.

"Come with me," Wes said, putting his arm around her and leading her to the living room couch. "I think you

should watch the reports. Right now they're the only information we have."

Sierra plopped down next to Randy and watched as
station after station replayed the horrifying scene of the
burning airplane on the runway. One station alluded to
terrorist activity. Another channel had an expert explain
how the recent strike of this particular airline could have
led to an oversight by the maintenance staff. CNN was
announcing it as the worst disaster in the Seattle airport's
history.

"Amy," Wes said after a while, "why don't you and I
pull some food together? We still have to eat. You guys just
kick back here, and Amy and I will take care of everything."

Eat? Sierra thought. *I couldn't possibly eat.*

Her dad sat on her right side and pulled her close.
Sierra rested her head on his arm. When she did, she caught
the faint scent of the soap he used. It was a green soap
that gave him a woodsy, outdoor fragrance. As soon as she
smelled it, she thought of Paul and his pine-tree aftershave,
which she had smelled for the first time when they sat next
to each other on the plane ride from San Francisco to
Portland. With the memory came a crashing wave of fresh
tears that Sierra unapologetically spilled all over her father's
chest.

Her friends stayed and ate tender lobster with drawn
butter on trays in front of the TV. Sierra didn't eat.

"I think we should pray together," Randy said after they
had seen footage of the crash at least 15 times. No new
reports of survivors were forthcoming, and in a way they
were all growing numb to the information, since it had

been well over an hour since they had heard the shocking news.

"Sometimes," Randy said, "it helps to have a verse to pray, you know? It helps to focus on God and His promises instead of being overwhelmed with the problem. I think it could help our prayers be more directed."

"In Paul's last letter, he wrote about Jesus being the Good Shepherd," Sierra offered.

"That's in John 10," Randy said.

Sierra's dad left the couch and returned a moment later with a Bible. "But that's a whole chapter, not just one verse," he said.

"It can be a whole chapter," Randy answered.

Then Sierra remembered the reference from Philippians that Paul had listed at the end of the letter. He had said it reminded him of her boldness. Sierra had looked up the verses once, but she couldn't remember now what they said.

"He also mentioned another verse in the first chapter of Philippians, near the end. Maybe verse 27," she told her dad.

He cleared his throat and read slowly, " 'Whatever happens to me, conduct yourselves in a manner worthy of the gospel of Christ. Then, whether I come and see you or only hear about you in my absence, I will know that you stand as one man for the faith of the gospel.' "

"Wow!" Margo said. "Is that the verse Paul wrote to you? It's kind of spooky that it says 'whatever happens to me.' "

"Actually, that's not the verse," Sierra said. The parallels between the apostle Paul's words in the letter to his Philippian friends and what was happening to Sierra after her letter from Paul MacKenzie were just a little too intense for her.

Then she remembered one of the verses Paul had listed in his letter. She had memorized it for Bible class and recognized it when Paul said he had written it on a card and carried it in his wallet. When she first had read the verse, it hadn't meant much to her, and she didn't understand why it was so important to Paul.

Now, as she was about to quote it to her dad and her friends, it took on special significance.

"I remember the verse," she said. "Philippians 1:21. 'For to me, to live is Christ and to die is gain.'"

chapter twelve

*S*IERRA'S FRIENDS HAD A HARD TIME PRAYING, BUT SHE didn't. She didn't care if her tears and overwhelming emotions soaked through her words. And she didn't care what anyone else thought of her. This was between her and God, and she was trying to make sense of this tragic news arriving on the tail of Paul's clear commitment to God.

"I know that Your ways aren't our ways, God. And I don't understand what's happening. Did You take Paul to heaven to be with You? Or is he still alive? God, I beg You to have mercy on him if he's still alive. All he wanted to do was serve You." Sierra felt exhausted. She stopped praying, and Randy stepped right in, as if holding up her arms when she was too weak to hold them up any longer.

Randy prayed for Paul's parents, Jeremy, Tawni, and Uncle Mac. He prayed for the doctors at the hospital and for all the families who had lost someone in the crash.

Mr. Jensen prayed, and then Tre. Tre's voice was calm and steady. He was so willing to accept whatever happened as being for God's best. Sierra wasn't so willing. Margo thanked God that Paul was a Christian and that therefore, if he were dead, they all would see him again in heaven.

That's when Amy left the room.

They prayed for more than half an hour. Randy's idea was a good one. It helped to focus on God's Word as they prayed. After the last "Amen," they sat still and looked at each other.

"Sierra," Margo said, "you should be ready to accept the worst because the worst is really the best. I mean, if Paul is dead, then he's with God. He's in heaven right now, and we're the ones who have to go through a lifetime of trials before we get set free the way he is."

Sierra wanted to blast her friend's easy answer and say she wasn't ready to accept Paul's death just like that. Fortunately, the doorbell rang.

"It's probably Vicki," Randy said. He rose to answer the door when Sierra didn't get up.

"Will you tell her?" Sierra asked Randy. "I don't think I can say it."

Randy nodded. They all heard him open the door. The sound of a party horn and the snap of a confetti streamer followed. Then they heard Vicki say loudly to Randy, "Look! I brought hats and party horns for everyone. You haven't had dessert yet, have you?" The party horn sounded again.

Sierra could hear Randy's muffled voice and then a gasp from Vicki. Vicki rushed into the living room and stared at Sierra as if she had to be sure this wasn't some kind of cruel joke. When Vicki saw Sierra, her face mirrored her friend's.

"No!" Vicki whispered, slumping to the floor at Sierra's feet. "I heard it on the radio on my way over, but I thought it couldn't be Paul's plane because he was coming into Portland." Slow tears began a procession down Vicki's cheeks. "Oh, Sierra, I'm so, so, so sorry."

"We don't know yet. He may be one of the survivors." Sierra tried to comfort her friend but found she didn't have as much hope as she had thought.

"Jeremy and Tawni drove up to Seattle with Uncle Mac," Randy explained. "They're going to call as soon as they get there."

Sierra felt parched and asked if anyone else wanted something to drink. No one did. She shuffled into the kitchen, which looked like a disaster area. It smelled fishy. The counter was covered with uneaten salads, baskets of bread, and a plateful of leftover lobster. For some reason she thought of the story of Jesus' feeding the crowd of more than 5,000 people with the simple offering of one little boy's fish and loaves. There had been 12 baskets of food left over, enough for each of Jesus' disciples to have his own basket.

As she poured herself a glass of water, Sierra tried to make a spiritual connection between that story and Paul's crisis. She needed to see a miracle and to know that God could take something small, like just a little bit of faith, and bless it and multiply it.

Then she remembered Paul's verse: "For to me, to live is Christ and to die is gain." What if the God-thing of all this was for Paul to be in heaven, and as a result, good would come out of his death?

The possibility was too brutal. God wouldn't do that, would He? Sierra leaned against the counter, realizing that whether or not Paul was one of the dead, 157 people had died today in that crash. Those 157 people had stepped into eternity. The ones who had surrendered their lives to God by receiving His gift of salvation through Christ were now in heaven. Those who had never come to Christ were now in hell.

Sierra felt like throwing up.

God, she screamed inside her mind, *how can You be like that? You divide us up like sheep and goats—right hand, left hand. I know what Your Bible says. I know what You require from us. But why? Couldn't You make it easier?*

As soon as the thought entered her mind, Sierra realized that coming to God was the easiest thing there was. Even a child could understand God's rules for eternal life and respond. It was a matter of choice, the free will God had put in each of us.

Her head was pounding. "Why don't people just come to You? Why do they run and hide and stay mad at You?"

Sierra hadn't realized she was saying that part of her wrestling match with God aloud until she heard Amy's soft voice answer from outside the open back door. "Because we're stubborn."

Sierra opened the screen and stepped out into the cool night. Amy sat on the steps with Brutus at her feet, contentedly letting Amy scratch under his chin.

"I didn't see you there." Sierra sat down next to her and patted Brutus on top of his noble head. "It's so hard, Aim. I mean, I know what I believe, and I'm sure it's right, but it's so severe. All those people dead. What did they do to deserve that?"

"We all deserve death," Amy said. "Have you already forgotten your verses from Bible class last year?"

Then, because all Sierra could give Amy was a blank look, Amy quoted them for her. " 'All have sinned and fall short of the glory of God. . . . The wages of sin is death, but the gift of God is eternal life in Christ Jesus our Lord.' "

"I know, but—"

Amy finished with one last verse. " 'The Lord is . . . not willing that any should perish but that all should come to repentance.' "

Sierra had no response. She knew all those verses, too. She had received an A on the test, just as Amy had. But what did they mean at a time like this? Amy knew the verses, but what did they mean to her?

"I think," Amy said, as if reading her friend's thoughts, "that the problem is in the repentance part. I haven't been willing to agree with God that I was wrong about anything. When my parents split up, all I knew was that I was hurting and nothing was going to make the hurt go away."

Sierra couldn't quite follow Amy's train of thought.

"I went my own way and tried to make myself feel better. It worked for a little while when I was with Nathan. But when you're in a dark place, there's no substitute for light."

The screen door opened. "There you are," Vicki said. She came and sat behind them. "I can't believe this is happening, Sierra. Do you really think he is, you know . . ."

"I don't know. Margo seems to think so. She said we

should be glad because we know he's in heaven and we'll see him again." Sierra choked up.

"Margo said that?" Vicki said.

"Isn't that what you believe?" Amy asked.

"Well, of course, but . . ." Vicki scooted closer and put her arm around Sierra. "This isn't exactly the time to say it. At least not that way."

"I believe it," Amy said. "Whether it's a convenient time or not, I know it's true."

Sierra and Vicki both looked at Amy and waited for her to explain this sudden confession of faith.

"For a long time," Amy said, tears gathering in her eyes, "it's as though I've been in a dungeon inside myself. It's been dark and cold and more miserable than I think either of you could ever guess. And I couldn't find the key. I couldn't get myself out of the dungeon. That's why I loved our Monday afternoons at Mama Bear's. It was as if you two came to visit me. You brought me a little bread, a little water, and some light from your two steady candles. And somehow I could keep going."

Sierra slipped her arm through Amy's and held her friend's hand, steady and calm, the way Randy had held hers. Vicki put her arm around Amy.

"I think I found the key that will get me out. I need to come back to God. All along I thought He was the one who locked me in there, but now I realize I was the one who locked Him out. I can't explain it, but I want God back."

"Then just tell Him," Sierra said, gently squeezing Amy's hand.

Amy didn't cry. She bowed her head with her two friends holding her, and she spoke simple, direct words, as only Amy could. "I've been wrong, God. I shut You out. I'm sorry. I want You back. Please forgive me and take me back. Okay?"

Then, as if Vicki could answer for God, she whispered back, "Okay."

The three of them opened their eyes and looked at each other warmly.

"Thanks for not giving up on me," Amy said quietly.

Sierra hugged her.

"Did I miss something earlier?" Vicki asked. "I mean, what happened, Amy?"

"What do you mean, what happened?"

Vicki looked at Sierra. "Did you say something to her?"

Sierra shook her head.

"You want to know why I suddenly opened my heart to God after shutting Him out for so long." Amy readjusted her position and looked at her friends. "It was the news report and the possibility that Paul might actually, you know . . . he could be dead right now."

Sierra felt an anxious surge of emotion begin to come over her again.

"When the news said there were three known survivors, something just hit me. It reminded me of the three of us. I wanted to be one of the survivors, not one of the 157."

Before Amy could say any more, the Jensen van pulled into the driveway. Mrs. Jensen, Granna Mae, and the boys came around to the back steps. Eager to greet them, Brutus rose and barked loudly. Mrs. Jensen instructed the boys to take Brutus to his doghouse so he wouldn't jump on Granna Mae.

"Well, hello!" Mrs. Jensen said when she saw the three friends clustered on the steps in the twilight. "Taking a break from the party?"

"Mom," Sierra began and then listened to herself tell about the plane crash and Tawni and Jeremy leaving with Uncle Mac.

Granna Mae stood at the bottom of the steps and listened quietly with her purse clutched in her hand. Sierra's mom breathed a troubled "Oh, dear" and leaned against the stair railing.

Granna Mae didn't move. She calmly said, "Paul wasn't on the plane."

Everyone turned to look at her, waiting for her to speak again.

"Paul missed the plane and went back to Saigon. That's when the bombing began."

Sierra understood then that Granna Mae was having one of her flashbacks. This one was about her son Paul, who had been killed in Vietnam. Her Paul had missed his plane ride, but the thought caused a fresh hope to spring up inside Sierra.

"What if Paul wasn't on the plane that crashed?" she said, excitedly springing up. "I mean, they changed his flight once already; maybe they changed it again. Maybe he didn't get on that flight!"

"Oh, Sierra," Mrs. Jensen said, reaching for her arm. But Sierra was already sprinting up the steps. "Dad? Wesley?" They met her in the kitchen. "Can we call the airline and check the flight roster? What if Paul wasn't on that flight?"

Mrs. Jensen and the others from outside were now in the kitchen, too. Sierra could tell that her mom and dad were exchanging glances and trying to signal to each other that their fairy-tale dreamer of a daughter was about to be disappointed. But Wesley didn't hesitate. He reached for the phone and started to make calls until he found someone who would help him.

As the whole group stood in the kitchen, waiting for the answer, Wes talked to the supervisor at the airline. Wes went through the story for the fourth time. He held up a hand for everyone to be quiet. "Can you repeat that, please? No, I don't believe he could have registered under a different name. It would have been listed as Paul MacKenzie. Yes, I'll wait."

Painful, silent moments passed.

"You're sure," Wes said. "Okay. Thank you. Yes. Good night." He hung up and turned to face Sierra. "He said Paul had a reservation on the flight, but according to their computer, he never checked in."

A wild cheer of amazement and jubilation rose from the group.

"He wasn't on the plane!" Sierra practically shouted, looking around for Granna Mae. The dear, confused woman must have gone to her room. It struck Sierra with painful clarity that because Granna Mae's Paul had missed his plane, he had met with death. But perhaps Sierra's Paul had missed death because he had missed a plane.

The phone rang, and Wes silenced the chatter before

answering it. "Yes, Jeremy, listen. Before you tell me any-thing, I have something to tell you. We called the airline, and Paul wasn't on the flight. He had a reservation, but he never received a seat assignment, and according to their computer, he never boarded the plane."

Sierra's heart was pounding. She wanted to grab the phone from Wes and tell Jeremy herself.

"Yes. I know. You did? And did you reach them? Oh, really. Okay. Well, are you coming back, then? Sure." Wes held the phone out to his dad. "Tawni wants to talk to you."

"What did you find out?" Sierra asked the minute Wes let go of the phone. "He wasn't at the hospital, right?"

Wes nodded. "He wasn't at the hospital, and he's not on the list of the confirmed fatalities. Jeremy still can't reach his parents. He called some of their friends, who said his parents had gone to their mountain cabin for the week-end. They don't have a phone there, so Jeremy asked the friends to drive up and tell them."

"What are they going to tell them?"

"I guess that Paul's okay."

"Is he?" Sierra asked. "I mean, he wasn't on the plane; he isn't here." Sierra looked around and wondered why she was the only one asking this question. "So, where is he?"

chapter thirteen

WES GRABBED THE PHONE FROM HIS DAD BEFORE
he hung up with Jeremy and said, "Jeremy,
Sierra just made a good point. Where *is* Paul?"

It was quiet for a moment. Sierra bit her lower lip and
tried to imagine what had happened to Paul. For all they
knew, he could have taken a different flight, and he could
be at the Portland airport right now, waiting for Uncle Mac
to pick him up.

"Okay, call us if you hear anything," Wes said before
hanging up. He then gave everyone in the room a rundown
on the plan. "Jeremy is going to call his grandmother in
Scotland to find out when Paul left her house. They're
going to drive back here and stop halfway to call for an
update. The friends who are going to the MacKenzies's
cabin have our number, and they'll call here, too."

"He's probably stuck at the airport in London," Vicki
said. "I'll bet he missed his flight and is still trying to get
another one. Or maybe he's already in the air and will call
when he arrives in Portland—or Seattle or wherever his
plane is going to land."

Just the words "Seattle," "plane," and "land" sent shivers up Sierra's spine.

"Sierra, you don't look very relieved," Vicki said. "Are you still in shock? Paul wasn't on the plane."

"I know," Sierra said.

"It's a lot to process so fast," Amy said, coming to Sierra's defense. "I'm like Sierra. I'll feel better when we know exactly where Paul is and why he missed the plane."

"It *is* a lot to process," Sierra said, pulling Amy to the side. The others had begun to help Wesley and Sierra's mom clean up the kitchen mess. "And your decision is a pretty huge event, too," Sierra said to Amy. "I don't want you to think I don't know how big a step that was for you. I'm so happy, Amy." Sierra tried but couldn't pull up a smile for her friend. "I'm deep down happy that you said what you did and that you let Vicki and me be there when you prayed. I've been praying for this for a long time."

"I know," Amy said quietly. "Thank you."

"So," Warner said, breaking into their twosome, "is it time to let the party begin? What happened to Vicki's hats and blowers?"

Sierra pulled herself out from under Warner's lumbering interference and went over to her dad. "Do you think we should go to the airport in case Paul comes in and doesn't have money to call Uncle Mac to pick him up?" A tiny smile came to her as she remembered how Paul hadn't been prepared with enough British coins for the phone when they had met at the London airport. He probably didn't have any American coins with him on this trip.

"I think he would find a way to call," Mr. Jensen said.

"We could be wandering around the airport for hours when he could still be stuck at Heathrow. It's better to wait here and keep in contact with people calling in."

Sierra nodded and meandered into the study. She shut the door behind her and took refuge in her favorite thinking chair. The study was dark, but she didn't turn on the light. Someone might realize she was there and come in. She needed to be alone, just for a few minutes.

Reviewing the available information, Sierra tried to put together the pieces. Paul could be anywhere. Then, silently moving her lips, with her eyes shut tight, Sierra prayed. For months she had prayed for Amy, and now, just like that, her prayers appeared to have been answered and Amy had come back to the Lord. For more than a year, she had prayed for Paul to turn wholeheartedly to God, and in just the last few weeks, he had. Sierra was so experienced at praying for her friends to come to Christ that she didn't know what to pray after they did.

Party sounds floated in from the kitchen. Everyone was relieved, and after all, this was supposed to be a celebration. But Sierra couldn't find a festive bone in her body at this moment. She knew she wouldn't feel like blowing any party horns until she knew where Paul was and that he was safe. Paul's image of Jesus as the Good Shepherd entered her thoughts. For the first time in her life, Sierra believed she had a tiny understanding of what it must be like for God to have lost sheep and to long for them all to come back to Him. She remembered the story of how the Good Shepherd left his flock of 99 safe sheep to search for the one lost sheep. He didn't end his search until that one was found and brought back safely.

"You brought Amy back," Sierra whispered to the Good Shepherd. "And You brought Paul back. Now please bring Paul back to me. Or, well, bring him back to his family and friends and bring him back safely. I know I can't pretend that I have any right to him. He's Your sheep. And so am I. I know You will lead us and guide us in the future, whether it's separately or together."

Sierra felt a calmness that had been missing during the last few hours of panic. She thought of her frustrated prayer earlier when Randy had gathered the group together. She had said then that God's ways weren't her ways and she was having a hard time understanding those ways. Right now, it seemed she didn't need to understand. All she needed to do was trust.

Before she left the study, Sierra drew in a deep breath. She noticed her lower lip was swollen and wondered how many times she had chewed on it during the last few hours without realizing it. A smile came to her as she thought of how terrible she was going to look when she finally did see Paul. Her lip would be swollen, and her eyes would probably still be red and puffy. Her chin was likely to break out within the next 12 hours. It usually did that when she was under stress and eating a lot of sugar.

The thought of sugar piqued Sierra's interest in eating. She had skipped lunch in all the graduation excitement and then had felt no interest in food when the lobster was served in front of the TV. Right now she could eat about anything.

Sierra's mom and Amy were the only two still in the kitchen when Sierra left the study and joined them. Mrs. Jensen's hands were submerged in soapy dishwater. She turned to Sierra and with a concerned look asked, "How are you doing?"

"I'm okay," Sierra said. "I'm actually kind of hungry."

"That's a good sign. What are you hungry for?"

"I don't know. I'll find something."

Sierra's "something," under Amy's creative direction, turned out to be a lobster sandwich. She cut open one of the dinner rolls and loaded it with lobster and sliced cherry tomatoes. It was even tastier than she imagined it would be.

Sierra found out that while she was in the study, Drake and Cassie had come by, and most of Sierra's guests had left with them to go to another party. She couldn't blame them. This hadn't exactly turned into the evening of enchantment she had planned. The only people left were Amy, Vicki, Randy, and Wes. Sierra's younger brothers had gone to bed. Her parents went upstairs but said they would stay up and wait for news.

Vicki went to her car and brought back a bag filled with yearbooks. They reminisced about Royal Academy and talked about it as if all the things that had happened to them there had taken place a decade ago. Sierra certainly felt she had lived a decade in the last five hours.

The phone rang, and Wes grabbed it. "She's right here," he said and handed the phone to Sierra.

"Hi, Sierra?" It was a deep, male voice. For one second her heart rose, thinking it might be Paul. "It's Drake."

"Oh," she said. Then she quickly added, "Hi."

"Margo just told me about Paul, and I wanted to call and see how you were doing."

"Thanks," Sierra said, pulling away from the group on the living room floor.

Vicki grabbed her leg and mouthed the word, "Paul?"

Sierra shook her head. "It's Drake," she said, covering the mouthpiece.

"Are you okay?" Drake asked. "Margo said you took it pretty hard. I saw the crash on the news. I can see how it would have rocked your world."

"It did," Sierra agreed. "We still haven't heard from Paul, so we don't know where he is. Tawni and Jeremy went to Seattle. They should be back in a couple of hours. I don't know if they'll have any more news or not."

"Well, I just wanted to call you and say happy gradu-ation, and I hope everything turns out with Paul and you."

"Thanks, Drake. I really appreciate that."

"I also wanted to say I appreciated what you wrote in my yearbook. I think you'll always hold a memorable spot in my life, too. I don't have any backpack trips planned this summer, but if I did, I'd want you along for the hike."

"That was an interesting trip, wasn't it?"

"Interesting," Drake repeated.

There was a pause before Drake said, "Well, I, um, I don't know if I'll see you much this summer, so have a good one and maybe we'll run into each other."

"I imagine we will," Sierra said, not sure why Drake would suddenly be so nice to her. He certainly appeared sincere.

"Take care, then. And I hope everything is okay with Paul."

"Thanks, Drake."

He hung up, and she returned to her circle of friends.

"What was that all about?" Amy asked.

Sierra shrugged. "Drake wanted to tell me he hoped everything turned out okay with Paul."

The phone rang again while it was still in Sierra's hand. She jumped before pushing the "On" button. "Hello?"

"Sierra, it's me," Tawni said. "Have you heard anything from Jeremy's parents?"

"Not yet."

"We finally reached his grandmother in Scotland. That was no easy task. She said Paul left last Tuesday because he was going to travel on a rail pass for a few days before he left the country."

Sierra relayed the message to Wesley and the others, who were waiting eagerly, before she answered Tawni. "That means he could be anywhere."

"Exactly. Jeremy is more concerned now, I think, than he was before. Paul would check in; this isn't like him."

"Maybe he tried to call his parents, but they were already in the mountains," Sierra suggested.

"You're right." Sierra could hear Tawni relaying the information to Jeremy and Uncle Mac. Then she said, "Jeremy, does anyone have a key to your parents' house who could listen to their answering machine?"

Jeremy's response was muffled. Sierra heard a loud page in the background.

"Where are you?" she asked.

"We're at the airport. When you guys discovered that Paul wasn't on the flight, Jeremy thought we should come here to see if Paul took another plane out of Heathrow. We've been checking with all the airlines for the past hour, but none of them has Paul listed on any of the flights."

"So he's probably still in London," Sierra surmised.

"That's what Uncle Mac thinks. He's making a few calls right now to see if he can have Paul paged at Heathrow, just in case Paul is stuck there, trying to get a flight out. Oh wait," Tawni said. The sound of muffled voices was drowned by another loud airport page, causing Sierra to hold the phone away from her ear as she explained to the others what Tawni had said.

"Sierra?"

"Yes, I'm still here."

"Uncle Mac didn't get a response to his page at Heathrow."

"What do you think that means?"

"Jeremy thinks Paul never arrived at the airport. He thinks he disappeared somewhere between his grand-mother's house and the airport. He could be anywhere."

Like a storm cloud, Tawni's words blew in and settled over Sierra's heart. With the swiftness of a lightning bolt, the intense pain Sierra had experienced earlier suddenly returned, striking her this time in the throat. She handed the phone to Wes and lowered herself into a chair.

For the first time ever, a jagged thought pierced her. *I might never see Paul MacKenzie on this earth again.*

chapter fourteen

SIERRA DIDN'T LIKE THE THOUGHTS THAT HOVERED over her throughout the long night. She tried to make them go away. She tried to reason them through. Nothing seemed to help. All she knew was that Paul MacKenzie probably wasn't dead. He was missing. For some reason, that was much more terrifying to wrestle with.

Randy went home around 2:00 in the morning. Amy and Vicki stayed. The three girls put out sleeping bags on the living room floor and changed into shorts and T-shirts. They waited all night for the phone to ring.

At a little past 4:00 in the morning, the phone finally rang. Sierra jumped to answer it, but the cordless wouldn't respond to her push of the button. The battery had gone out again.

"Somebody get the phone!" she yelled, scrambling for the phone in the kitchen. She grabbed it on the fifth ring. All she heard was a click and some static. The answering machine was set to pick up calls on the fifth ring, so Sierra ran into the study to grab the phone connected to the answering machine.

"Hello?" She could hear her father's recorded message playing over the line. "Wait just a second," she said.

The voice on the other line sounded like a recording also. Sierra listened hard to decipher what it was saying.

"Hello?" Wesley's voice came over the upstairs extension.

"Hang up, Wesley. The phones are all messed up."

"What?"

More static.

"Hang up!" Unfortunately, whoever was on the other end must have thought the command was for him, and he hung up.

"Sierra?" Wesley said.

Frustrated, she hung up the phone and went back into the kitchen to hang up that extension. Wes came bounding down the stairs, along with Sierra's dad.

"Who was it?"

"Our phones are messed up!" Sierra stated, pushing her hair out of her face. "If it rings again, only one person should answer it. I really think it could have been Paul."

Vicki and Amy appeared from the living room; Amy was holding the dead cordless phone.

"Are you sure?" Mr. Jensen asked Sierra.

Sierra felt like crying. "I'm not sure of anything. I tried to get it before the answering machine picked it up and then . . ." Before Sierra could finish, a clear thought broke through her deep blue funk. "The answering machine!"

She turned and headed back to the study. The confused troop followed her.

"Did anyone ever listen to the messages?" Sierra bent over the machine and pushed the rewind button.

They heard a beep, and then an electronic-sounding voice said, "This is the overseas operator. Will you accept a collect call from . . ." There was a click and then in his own voice they heard Paul say, "Paul MacKenzie." A pause followed as the electronic overseas operator tried to discern if the answer to its question was "yes" or "no." Of course all the answering machine gave was silence as the tape rolled, so the mechanical operator hung up.

"No," Sierra cried. "Why did it do that? Where is he? When did he call?"

The next message beeped, and the group fell silent again to listen. It was the same mechanical operator, only this time, instead of Paul saying his name, he listed some numbers. Again, when there was no answer, the "operator" hung up.

"He's trying to leave you a message," Amy said. "Those numbers! Play it back, and write down the numbers. You can call them and see if he's there."

It seemed a little strange to Sierra's dad, but Sierra agreed with Amy. If Paul realized he couldn't get the phone to take a message, he had to use whatever means he could to communicate with them. Sierra wondered if Paul had tried to reach his parents as well but only got their machine. Uncle Mac had been at the airport waiting for Paul, so it was possible Paul hadn't been able to reach him yesterday afternoon, either.

Sierra replayed the message while Wes wrote down the numbers. They tried phoning them only to hear a recording that said their call couldn't go through as dialed.

"It's probably a London number," Sierra said. "Don't we have to dial another number first to get international access? I know there's a code for each country in Europe."

"I'll call the operator," Wes said.

"It'll be a machine," Vicki predicted.

But it was an actual person, and Wes set to work, trying to solve the mystery. The operator tried seven different possibilities, but none of those seven codes with the numbers Paul left was the right combination. They tried one more, and Wesley looked up excitedly.

"I have a connection. It's ringing." He held up his hand, motioning for silence. "Yes, hello," he said into the receiver. "What did you say this was? Danbury House? Yes, well, I'm not sure I have the correct number. Pardon me? Yes, I am calling from the U.S. I'm trying to contact Paul MacKenzie. By any chance is he there?"

Sierra held her breath and bit her lower lip.

"Yes, I understand. Could you check your roster, though, and see if his name appears? Oh, I see. Yes."

"What?" Sierra begged to know, tugging on Wesley's arm.

"So he left this morning, and you don't expect him to return," Wesley repeated. "Do you know if he was planning to go to the airport? Did he say anything about flying back home today?"

It was silent far too long.

"Yes. I understand. Thank you. Good-bye."

"What?" Sierra asked before Wes had even hung up the phone.

"The Danbury House is some sort of homeless shelter in London. Paul checked in last night and left this morning. She said he had to go to the free clinic to get some stitches."

"Stitches?" they all repeated.

Before they could get any more information from Wes, Tawni and Jeremy arrived, looking exhausted.

"Paul's in London," Sierra announced. "He tried to call here. Is Uncle Mac in the car?"

"He dropped us off. What did you find out?"

Wes relayed the story and added the details the others were waiting for. "Apparently, Paul arrived last night with some cuts on his face. They cleaned him up, gave him some food and a bed, and sent him to a clinic this morning. The woman I talked to remembered Paul. She talked about him as if he were a common street bum."

Sierra began to put together the pieces. "He must have been mugged," she surmised. "The robber beat him up and took everything, which is why Paul couldn't take the plane home yesterday. And they took his money, so that's why he's calling collect."

The others looked at her as if she had an overly active imagination.

"It fits," Jeremy was the first to say. "If his passport was taken, that would explain why he didn't leave England yet."

"Where would he go to get a new passport?" Tawni asked.

"The American Embassy," Sierra said. She had traveled to Europe twice and had learned enough to know what to do in an emergency. "Let's call there and leave a message for him."

Jeremy called this time. Mr. Jensen retreated to the kitchen to start a pot of coffee, nice and dark, the way he liked it. Sierra and the others waited. Tawni flopped onto the living room couch and told them to wake her as soon as there was some news.

Twenty minutes later, Jeremy met with success. He reached the embassy and found out that Paul had been there earlier and had registered all the necessary forms. The agent at the embassy wouldn't give out any further information, such as whether or not the passport had been stolen. They still didn't know where he was, but at least he was okay.

Sierra felt as if she could begin to breathe again, and she drew in generous lungsful of air. The smell of her dad's strong coffee filled her nostrils, and she decided to try half a cup, mixed with lots of cream and sugar. Paul had dreamed of drinking good coffee again, and now that they knew he was okay, Sierra felt she could start the celebration before he arrived.

At 5:00 the phone rang. Sierra answered, and it was Uncle Mac saying he had just received a collect call from Paul, and he was all right. Sierra quickly told him everything they had figured out, and Mac said, "Good detective work, Sherlock! You pretty much figured it out. He got off a bus in London in the wrong district. He had stayed the night at a youth hostel and was trying to take the bus to the airport to catch his flight. When he realized he was on the wrong bus, he got off, hoping to catch the next one. It was a bad area, and no cabs were around for him to hail. He said he waited at the bus stop for more than an hour, but no bus came. He asked someone for directions and took off walking, which was probably his second mistake. The directions led him down an alley, and that's where the hoodlums got him. It was as if they were lying in wait for him, he said."

"Did they hurt him?" Sierra asked.

"Yes. They knocked him down and took everything: his backpack, wallet, money, passport. I think he said he had four stitches put in his chin this morning at a clinic."

"This is so awful!" Sierra said.

The others were gathering around Sierra, waiting for an update. She motioned that she would tell them everything in just a minute.

"I was able to wire him some money," Uncle Mac said. "At least he can find something to eat and buy some shoes. They took his shoes, and he's been walking around London barefoot."

Sierra couldn't imagine what Paul had been through. But at least he was safe. And he would be home soon.

"How long will it take him to get his passport?" Sierra asked.

"He didn't say. He's going to try to reach his parents today and figure out his ticket home. I told him his folks were at the cabin but to keep trying them because they were heading home. If he doesn't contact them by tonight his time, I told him to call me back and I'd work out the ticket with him."

"Did he sound okay?" Sierra asked. "I mean, was he feeling all right?"

"You'll be able to tell me in a little while," Uncle Mac said. "I told him to call you and Jeremy at your house and to charge it to my account. I'd better get off the line because he was going to wait 20 minutes and then give you a call."

Sierra hung up and gave the group the update. Everyone responded at once.

"He could have been killed."

"I'm so glad he's okay."

"Barefoot? Through London? No thank you."

"When is he going to call?"

"Any minute," Sierra said, checking the clock on the microwave. She sipped her overly sweetened, cooled coffee and decided it wasn't worth the effort.

The first streaks of morning had broken into the kitchen, bringing a sense of comfort and hope to the weary bunch. Mr. Jensen decided to make a batch of scrambled eggs. Jeremy helped him with the toast, and Amy unloaded the dishwasher so Wesley would have glasses for the orange juice he was making. Sierra sat and watched, waiting for the phone to ring. She realized no one had told Tawni the good news, so Sierra slipped into the living room and woke her sister.

"Paul's okay. He's in London. He was robbed."

Tawni raised up on her elbow and squinted. "He was robbed?"

"Yes, but he's all right. He's trying to get another passport and a ticket home."

"That's awful!"

"No, it's good," Sierra said. "He's alive. He's coming home."

"I'm so glad," Tawni said, lying back down. "Do you mind if I go back to sleep?"

"Not at all. Do you want to go upstairs to bed?"

"No. I just want to . . ." Tawni's voice trailed off, and she was back asleep.

Sierra returned to the kitchen, trying not to appear too frustrated that the phone hadn't rung yet. Mr. Jensen was beginning to dish up the eggs, so she grabbed a paper plate and let him pile it on. The conversation swirled around the weary bunch. No one but Sierra seemed nervous that the phone hadn't rung. She could barely stand the suspense. There was so much she wanted to ask Paul.

At 7:10 the phone finally rang. Vicki and Amy had gone home. Wes had fallen asleep in a chair in the living room. Jeremy had crashed on the living room floor. Sierra and her dad were the only two still awake. Mr. Jensen had gone outside to work in the yard while it was cool, and Sierra was cleaning the kitchen. It was a good outlet for her nervous energy. She had even mopped the floor, since it was sticky where the buckets of lobsters had rested the night before.

She answered the phone, breathless from the mopping.

"Good morning," the male voice said. "I apologize for calling so early. This is Pastor MacKenzie. Is my son Jeremy there?"

"Yes; I'll get him." Sierra felt like the maid, standing there with the mop in her hand and her hair twisted up and held on top of her head with a clip. She had waited so patiently for Paul to call, but here it was his dad instead, and he had no idea who Sierra was or why she was important to his son.

Sierra woke Jeremy and said, "Your dad is on the phone. You'd better take it in the kitchen or the study because the cordless isn't working right."

Jeremy shook himself awake and stretched his long arms over his head as he went into the kitchen. "Dad?" he said, taking the phone. "Yeah. I'm fine. What have you heard?"

Sierra remained inconspicuous in the background while Jeremy and his dad compared notes on Paul's situation. She gathered from a few of the comments Jeremy made that Paul had obtained a ticket and could use it as soon as his new passport was issued. Jeremy hung up and turned to see if Sierra was still in the kitchen.

She looked up sheepishly, as if she had been caught eavesdropping. Jeremy walked over to where she stood wiping off the counter for the ninth time. He looked so compassionate and understanding that she knew something was wrong.

"What?" she said. "What is it? Is Paul okay?"

Jeremy nodded. "He's okay. But his ticket is a direct flight to San Diego. He won't be able to come through Portland."

"Oh," Sierra said, trying to appear brave. "That's understandable."

"I'm sorry," Jeremy said, putting a brotherly hand on her shoulder. "I know how much you were looking forward to seeing him."

chapter fifteen

*J*EREMY'S COMMENT STAYED WITH SIERRA FOR THE next three days as she floated in a deep blue funk, waiting for the phone to ring and for the voice on the other end to be Paul's. But he didn't call.

Sierra had time on her hands, since school was out and she had taken off these days from work. She had intended to fill the time with an unending list of adventures with Paul. Instead, she spent most of the days in her room alone, thinking of how Jeremy had tried to comfort her when he said, "I know how much you were looking forward to seeing him."

Did he mean that I was looking forward to being with Paul more than Paul was looking forward to being with me? she thought. *Jeremy read the letter. He saw how much Paul cares.*

Every now and then, Sierra could cheer herself up with the thought that Paul had several complications in his life at the moment and that he would call her when he arrived home. She was being unfair to expect a phone call when the poor guy was traipsing barefoot through London with four stitches in his chin. He had places to go, things to buy, tickets to book.

Still, she wondered how hard it would be to find a phone, use his uncle's charge number, and call her. Two minutes—that's all she needed. A two-minute call that said, "I'm fine. I'm sorry I didn't get to see you. I'll come up to Portland as soon as I can." Two minutes—that's all it would take. And then her life could go on again.

Tawni and Jeremy had left Sunday morning. Tawni's roommate had called and said a photo shoot was scheduled for Tawni on Tuesday morning that her agent had forgotten to tell her about. They left in a hurry, both tired and not looking forward to the two-day drive home. Sierra felt sorry for her sister, since she knew she had a hard time sleeping in the car. Tawni would probably end up splitting the driving with Jeremy when she had planned on Jeremy and Paul doing all the driving.

Wesley had gone back to Corvallis, where he was taking a summer-school course and working at a grocery store. Sierra missed her brother and sister more than she thought she would. In that one emotion-packed weekend, Sierra, Tawni, and Wesley had become closer than ever. Part of it might have been due to Sierra's graduating. Now she officially was a member of the older Jensen children group instead of the oldest member of the younger Jensen children group. In addition, the three of them had stood beside Jeremy as he had faced the possibility of losing his brother, and that had made them process all their feelings for each other.

Randy came by twice to try to convince Sierra that she

should do something with the rest of the gang. She just didn't feel like it, and Randy seemed to understand.

Vicki and Amy seemed to understand her depression, too. Vicki had called at 4:00 on Monday afternoon to suggest that Sierra meet with Vicki and Amy at Mama Bear's. Sierra told Vicki she just didn't feel like it yet.

"Are you still waiting for him to call?" Vicki asked.

Sierra didn't answer. She felt childish waiting around for the phone to ring when she should be out having a great time now that she had graduated.

"Have you heard if he's arrived in San Diego yet? I mean, did he get home safely?"

"I haven't heard. I don't think Tawni is home yet. I'll call her tomorrow."

"Well, do you want to do something on Wednesday?" Vicki asked. "I don't have to work until noon that day. We could meet for breakfast or something."

"Sure," Sierra agreed.

Now it was Wednesday, and she was on her way to meet Vicki and Amy for breakfast. She still had received no news of Paul. Tawni hadn't returned her calls; Sierra guessed Tawni was out on a shoot. For all Sierra knew, Paul could still be in London, waiting for a new passport.

In some ways, she had moved past the emotional churning of the weekend and had grown in the process. She had slept long hours and had thought deep and hard about life and death, love and pain. She had written a lot in her diary, read a lot in her Bible, and talked a lot with her dad.

When she arrived at Mama Bear's Bakery, Vicki and

Amy were waiting for her at their favorite window table. Just seeing her friends' smiling faces as she walked up to the bakery made Sierra's spirits feel lighter. She realized nothing was better in this life than friends who were there for her when she needed them.

Mrs. Kraus called to Sierra from behind the counter before she had a chance to join Vicki and Amy. "Could you come here a minute?"

Sierra joined Mrs. Kraus at the register. No customers were waiting for cinnamon rolls at the moment. "I was going to call you, so I'm glad you stopped by. Jody gave her notice yesterday."

"Oh, that's too bad. I'm going to miss her."

"Yes," Mrs. Kraus said, "we'll all miss Jody. But lots of hours are now up for grabs, and I wanted to tell you, since you had been asking about more hours this summer."

"That's perfect. Yes, I'll take whatever you can give me. But you remember, don't you, that I'll be here only until the second week of August?"

"Yes. And I'll miss you, too. But until then I'll give you most of Jody's hours, and you can earn some spending money for your college days."

"Thank you so much."

"My pleasure." Mrs. Kraus smiled. "Peppermint tea this morning?"

Sierra nodded and went over to join her friends. "Did you guys already order?"

"We're each having our own cinnamon roll today," Amy said. "Mrs. Kraus said a fresh batch would be out in five minutes, so we're waiting."

"Guess what?" Vicki's smile was wide.

"I don't know," Sierra said. "But I have a 'guess what' for you, too. Mrs. Kraus is giving me more hours. Now that is a huge God-thing."

"And this is a huge God-thing, too," Vicki said, still smiling. She pulled a legal-sized envelope from her purse.

Before Sierra saw the return address, she knew. "You were accepted at Rancho!" She threw her arms around Vicki in a hug. "I knew it! I knew it!"

Vicki laughed. "How did you know?"

"Because they can't break us up. We need each other too much." As soon as Sierra said it, she realized she had excluded Amy from the "we." "I mean . . ."

"It's okay," Amy said. "I guess I have a God-thing for both of you."

Vicki and Sierra waited. Amy had never referred to anything in her life as a God-thing before.

"Yesterday I sent in my application for Rancho. I guess I felt the same way you do, Sierra. They can't break us up. Besides, I've forgotten all the reasons I didn't want to go to a Christian college."

Sierra and Vicki were out of their chairs, hugging Amy and both talking at once. Mrs. Kraus showed up with the cinnamon rolls and tea, and they settled back in the chairs.

"You know what?" Amy spoke softly. "I feel as if I've changed so much in the past . . . what, how many days has it been since I prayed with you guys? Five days? Six now? I feel . . . I don't know—put back together or something."

"That is so great, Amy," Sierra said. "I feel as if I've been on a soul search, too, these past few days. I don't know if I feel put back together yet, but I'm getting there."

"You'll probably feel better once you hear from Paul and know that he's safe," Vicki said.

Sierra agreed and put the first bite of warm cinnamon roll into her mouth. The gooey frosting clung to her lower lip, and she wiped it with her napkin. Then Sierra looked out the window and noticed her mom coming toward Mama Bear's with something in her hand.

As her mom entered the bakery, Sierra immediately said, "Is everything okay?"

Mrs. Jensen smiled. "A courier just delivered this. It's from Paul, and I'll be honest, I couldn't wait for you to get home to open it."

They all laughed. Sierra took the second-day international mail envelope from her mom and coyly said, "What makes you think I'm going to open it in front of you guys?"

They all protested at once. Sierra said, "Okay, okay. Just let me read it first in private, okay?" She pulled out a single sheet of stationery from a hotel called The Edwina Courtyard and skimmed it quickly. The letter directed her to something else in the envelope, which she pulled out. It was small, thin, and wrapped in a single piece of tissue.

"What is it?" Amy asked.

"What did the letter say?" Vicki asked.

Sierra ignored them just long enough to pull back the tissue. She extracted a long chain with a silver emblem hanging from it.

"A daffodil," Mrs. Jensen said, reaching over to finger the dainty necklace. "It's beautiful, Sierra."

"Put it on," Amy urged.

Sierra slipped it over her head and adjusted the daffodil so that the finely detailed lines were showing. She grinned at her mom and then at Amy and Vicki. "Do you want to hear the letter?"

"Oh, no, that's okay," Vicki teased.

"I want to hear it," Mrs. Jensen said, moving in closer.

Dear Daffodil Queen [Sierra began],

What a weekend! I honestly hope yours was better than mine. However, after I heard about the crash in Seattle, I realized my experience wasn't so bad. Do you think sometimes God allows uncomfortable things to happen so that other, worse things won't happen? I've learned so much these past few days. I am convinced that, when we are God's own, we are indestructible until He is finished with us. Bad things happen to us, true. The storms come. But none of His sheep is ever out of His care.

I've enclosed your graduation gift. I had it made in the village where my grandmother lives. It's a daffodil, as you can see. It represents your bold spirit, Sierra— the way you brightly proclaim the truth. I had the chain made extra long so you could wear it next to your heart.

Now, I have to tell you, I intended to buy a proper box and wrap it before I gave it to you. However, since I didn't have a box, I wore the necklace while I was in London. It's about the only thing that wasn't taken from me. Perhaps they didn't notice it inside my shirt, next to my heart.

"Oh," Vicki said with a sigh, "this is the most romantic

letter in the world, Sierra. Can you believe the necklace wasn't stolen?"

The women exchanged looks of amazement.

"There's a little more," Sierra said, continuing to read.

> *Since I won't be coming to Portland, I wanted to get this necklace to you as quickly and safely as possible, so I'm sending it from London as I wait for my passport to clear. There's been a hitch over my visa, since I was on a student visa this past year in Scotland.*
>
> *When I finally arrive at my parents' house, I'll call you. Until then, may the peace of our good Shepherd be upon you.*
>
> *With hope and affection,*
> *Paul*

Sierra looked up. Her mom, Vicki, and Amy were gazing at her with soft, mushy-hearted expressions.

"I think I'm going to cry," Mrs. Jensen said.

Sierra felt embarrassed. She had never shared one of Paul's letters with her mother before. She wondered if Paul would mind that she had read his carefully crafted words in a public place to these women. Too late now. Looking down, Sierra gently rubbed her thumb over the silver daffodil. "It's beautiful, isn't it?"

Vicki leaned closer and admired the gift. "Forget everything Amy and I tried to teach you about guys. Whatever we learned from our past boyfriends is worthless. Whatever you're doing with Paul is working perfectly."

"I'm not 'doing' anything," Sierra said. "Except

praying. You know that. I've prayed for him since the day I met him."

Amy grinned. "I predict an improvement in Vicki's prayer life this summer!"

Vicki laughed. "If Randy mails me a guitar pick he once used to pick his teeth, we'll know that Sierra's formula works."

They all laughed.

"You girls are teasing, aren't you?" Mrs. Jensen said. "You do know there are no formulas when it comes to love. Praying for a guy doesn't guarantee he will suddenly become interested in you."

"Oh, Mom, we're only kidding," Sierra said, folding Paul's letter and tucking it back in the mailer.

"Just checking," Mrs. Jensen said with a grin. "I guess I should get going."

"No, stay," Amy pleaded.

"Yes, please stay," Vicki agreed.

Sierra hopped up. "I'll be right back with your very own cinnamon roll and a milk."

"Nonfat, please," her mom said.

"Okay! Nonfat milk with a 5,000-calorie cinnamon roll. That's going to make a big difference!" Sierra laughed all the way to the counter. As she walked, she could feel her new silver necklace tap lightly against her T-shirt. She fingered it again, feeling as bright, bold, and steady as the daffodil Paul had encountered on his hike.

It suddenly didn't matter that the weekend's events had

nearly crushed her. Paul was right. Storms do come. But after the storm comes a gentle calm like Sierra was feeling in her heart right then. In that calm, Sierra knew she and her good Shepherd were closer than ever.

Don't Miss These Captivating Stories in
THE SIERRA JENSEN SERIES

THE CHRISTY MILLER SERIES

If you've enjoyed reading about Sierra Jensen, you'll love reading about Sierra's friend Christy Miller.

#1 • Summer Promise
Christy spends the summer at the beach with her wealthy aunt and uncle. Will she do something she'll later regret?

#2 • A Whisper and a Wish
Christy is convinced that dreams do come true when her family moves to California and the cutest guy in school shows an interest in her.

#3 • Yours Forever
Fifteen-year-old Christy does everything in her power to win Todd's attention.

#4 • Surprise Endings
Christy tries out for cheerleader, learns a classmate is out to get her, and schedules two dates for the same night.

#5 • Island Dreamer
It's an incredible tropical adventure when Christy celebrates her sixteenth birthday on Maui.

#6 • A Heart Full of Hope
A dazzling dream date, a wonderful job, a great car. And lots of freedom! Christy has it all. Or does she?

#7 • True Friends
Christy sets out with the ski club and discovers the group is thinking of doing something more than hitting the slopes.

#8 • Starry Night
Christy is torn between going to the Rose Bowl Parade with her friends or on a surprise vacation with her family.

#9 • Seventeen Wishes
Christy is off to summer camp—as a counselor for a cabin of wild fifth-grade girls.

#10 • A Time to Cherish
A surprise houseboat trip! Her senior year! Lots of friends! Life couldn't be better for Christy until . . .

#11 • Sweet Dreams
Christy's dreams become reality when Todd finally opens his heart to her. But her relationship with her best friend goes downhill fast when Katie starts dating Michael, and Christy has doubts about their relationship.

#12 • A Promise Is Forever
On a European trip with her friends, Christy finds it difficult to keep her mind off Todd. Will God bring them back together?